ANNIE CONNELL

A BLIGHTED STAR

'Tis because we be on a blighted star,
and not a sound one, isn't it, Tess?'

THOMAS HARDY, TESS OF THE
D'URBERVILLES, 1891

Contents

BEA

I first met Bea at Starting Over Week. Everyone else there was a bit of a blur to me but Bea stood out. She was the kind of person that's hard to overlook, the kind of person whose presence hits you before you've had time to take in all of their physical features. At least, that's how she seemed to me. She didn't take up any more space than any other person. She was average height and a little lean and angular. Her features were regular and boyish. She had a flop of strawberry blond hair, a generous smattering of freckles and the most uncompromising eyes you ever saw. Cobalt-blue, they looked around and took in their surroundings with a palpable intensity. When she turned them on me, I felt like she was, no page-unturned, reading me. They seemed to be saying, 'We've seen all the bullshit this world has to give and we're fooled by none of it, including you.'

If I was right and she could see right through me, the first thing she would have noticed was that I didn't want to be there. The chores and some of the activities were okay but the counselling sessions were the last thing I wanted to be doing. I didn't want to do the individual sessions and I, sure as hell, didn't want to go to the group sessions. I didn't want to talk about what had happened to me and I didn't want to hear about all the crap that had happened to other people either. Knowing 'you're not alone' in going through something traumatic might be helpful for some, but hearing over and over about all the terrible things that have happened to other people wasn't my idea of a pick-me-up. All that I wanted to do was to be able to stop thinking about it.

I'd had to talk about it twice already. After it happened, I tried to keep it to myself and, while I had some control over that all the time that I was awake, as soon as I fell asleep the nightmares came and I couldn't stop myself crying out. Naturally, mum wanted to know what was wrong. To start with, I managed to fob her off saying I'd been watching too many scary movies. Scary movies didn't explain why I was making up mystery illnesses so that I wouldn't have to go to school though. Eventually, mum sat me down and said she wasn't going anywhere until I told her what was really going on. So, I told her and then one thing led to another and I had to tell Glen and, nice as he was about it, that was the most excruciating ninety minutes of my life. After that, they set me up for some online counselling but I wasn't about to expose myself again, especially not to some flat, jumpy person on a screen that I'd never even met. I just sat and looked at the poor woman and said nothing until she gave up, rang mum and said she didn't think that I was ready for it yet.

Months ticked by and I still wasn't in a good place and I could see that mum was really worried. I thought she'd forgotten all about counselling, though, but then one day she announced she'd found this residential course that might help me and please would I go, even if it was just for her. I didn't want to, of course, but she seemed to think the fact that it was still running and that they'd given me a place meant something significant and hopeful. She was even more convinced when she realised the course was going to be able to go ahead before the next lockdown descended on us. I wouldn't have gone but I wanted to please her. I could see that she was struggling too and she wasn't getting any help from anywhere. I figured the least I could do was pretend to be willing.

So, there I was, staying in a beautiful manor house in the middle of the countryside with several shell-shocked looking girls, a couple of equally unhappy looking boys and a team of mentors and Bea. The mentors were okay, I suppose. They were well-intentioned and they wanted to help, but I couldn't see the point of engaging with them at all. It wasn't like they could actually change what had happened.

They didn't enforce anything on us. Nothing was compulsory, especially not the counselling. Their strategy was to 'bond' with us, and earn our trust, during the other activities and at meal-times. My strategy was to do whatever I could to avoid them. On the first day, I explored the house and gardens looking for places that I'd be able to disappear into, if necessary. In the gardens there was an ice-house, a temple with convenient nooks and crannies, a bridge that I could get underneath and some trees that would be easy to climb really high and out-of-sight in. The house itself was huge with big landings and little staircases going all over the place. Most of it was closed off to us, though. We were supposed to stick to the dining room, downstairs, and the dormitory and a couple of other rooms on the first floor. None of it was very promising for hiding places. There was a ledge outside the dormitory window but it wasn't big enough to sit on safely. If it came to it, I was either going to have to hide outside or lock myself in the toilet.

I went to bed early the first night and got up late. I dawdled about and made sure I was the last one down to breakfast. The mentors were all enthusiastically chatting to other kids, or with each other, when I got there and I managed to find a quiet place to sit where no-one bothered me. Afterwards, when we had to help clear up, some woman called Leah or Laura or something tried talking to me and, I was polite and everything but, as soon as I could, I made my excuses and snuck outside. I went down the main steps and walked along until I found a little wall to sit on, and looked around.

I might not have wanted to be there but, I had to admit, it was an amazing place. A huge grassy area sloped down to the lake and there was woodland on either side. A strange collection of sculptures was dotted about on the lawn – metallic circles, stone figures and wooden blocks. That's when I first saw her. She was standing underneath a wooden block angel, inspecting it closely, and there was a golden retriever standing beside her.

She turned around and gazed in my direction and I looked away. She and the retriever walked up to me and she gave me the once over as I stroked the slobbery dog. 'I call him Trojan,' she said, 'because he's a Trojan dog. He's one of them and they use him to soften us up and gain our confidence. Whatever you do, don't trust him.'

4

I looked up at her, confused. She gave me one of her challenging looks and I sat there, dumbfounded, not knowing what to say. Just then the Leah/Laura woman came out looking for us. 'The introductory session is about to start in the blue room,' she told us. 'Do you want to come and see what it's all about?'

I looked at Bea who shrugged and said, 'Why not?' She followed Leah/Laura, I got up and followed her and Trojan followed me. At least, he did until we got indoors and then he padded off in the direction of the kitchen.

We were the last ones into the introductory session. Bea sat in the nearest empty chair to the door but I had to sit on the far side of the room. She grinned at me as I sat down and I gave her a half-smile back. A woman called Meena introduced herself and explained the timetable for the week and what she was hoping we might get out of it. After that, we were asked to say our names and anything else we wanted to share about ourselves. There were about sixteen of us in the room, altogether, so it took a while. Some people had a lot to say but I just said my name and so did Bea.

After the introductions we were supposed to be doing trust exercises, whatever that was. I felt my stomach start to churn and my palms begin to sweat as one of the other mentors explained the activity. I looked around in a panic and then I noticed that, opposite me, Bea was rolling her eyes and jerking her head frantically towards the door. Her eyebrows rose up in a big question mark when she saw that I'd finally noticed. I nodded and then waited for her to stand up. I was glad of the opportunity to cut but I wasn't confident enough to be the first one to do it.

Bea was first out of the door and she waited for me at the top of the stairs. As soon as I caught up with her, she grabbed my hand and we ran. We ran down and around the grand, swirling staircase and out through the huge front doors. We ran down the steps and all the way down the lawn, weaving through the sculptures, until we got to the lake. Once there, we slipped off our shoes and tip-toed to the end of the little jetty, where we sat with our feet dangling in the water. I laid back on the jetty and basked in the warmth of the morning sun. 'Thanks,' I said, and rolled onto one side. 'This feels great.' And it did. Even though I knew I was allowed to leave that room, running away from it like that gave me a feeling of control and lightness that I'd not felt in a long time.

I sat up again and beamed at Bea. 'Do you think there's a monster living in this lake?' she asked, as she tried to catch a frond of lakeweed between her toes. I looked across at the ducks and swans swimming around on the far side and then into the clear water beneath us.

'It doesn't look like the kind of lake that would have anything too weird or wonderful living in it,' I replied. 'Do you believe in lake monsters and stuff like that then?'

'I think so,' she said. 'I like the idea of them. My aunt lives up in Inverness and, when I'm eighteen, I'm going to go and live with her. Then I'm going to try and find the Loch Ness Monster.'

'That sounds fun. I'd really like to do something like that,' I said.

'She says I can go up there now if I want to,' continued Bea, 'but there's things I need to do here before I move.'

I waited for her to elaborate but she didn't and I didn't feel like I should ask. Instead, I looked down into the lake and then startled when a foot-long orange and white fish broke the surface of the water just a few feet in front of us. 'Does that count as a monster?' I asked Bea.

She shook her head. 'That's a koi,' she said, knowledgeably. 'Not quite as good as a monster but still, pretty cool. Are there any more?'

We spent the rest of the afternoon looking for big fish and talking about all the mythical creatures we'd ever heard of. Turned out, Bea was quite an expert on yetis and gorgons and minotaurs and furies. Sitting there in the hot sun with the water cooling our feet, I realised I was glad that mum had pushed me into this. Bea was fun to hang out with and, best of all, it was really nice to be with someone who wasn't looking at me with worried eyes or asking me questions that I didn't want to answer.

After that, Bea and I were inseparable. We did our chores and activities together and skipped off during the counselling sessions. We explored the woods or borrowed the house bikes and a couple of times we cycled into the village for sweets and chocolate. The village was pretty small. There were a few brick cottages either side of the main road and a little green in the middle. There was a craft shop called 'The Penny Farthing' and the village store where we bought our supplies. In the middle of the green, there was one of those big, red telephone boxes with the heavy doors. This one was full of old books and games and had a sign saying 'Help Yourself' inside it. Bea loved it.

The second time we went, she spent a long time in the phone box looking through all the books. I sat outside with the bikes and ate bon-bons, while I waited for her. All of a sudden, a grey hatchback screeched to a halt on the other side of the green and four boys piled out of it. As they headed for the shop, they leered and gawked at me. The tallest boy wolf-whistled and a pudgy, pale-faced boy shouted something about 'the tits on that.'

Bea shot out of the phone box and glared at the backs of the boys as they disappeared into the shop. 'Come on,' she said. 'Let's go. Are you alright?' I nodded and we started cycling back.

We'd gone about half a mile when we heard the roar of an engine and the grey car tore past us. It squealed a three-point turn at the next junction and made a beeline back towards us, on the wrong side of the road. Then the driver brought the car up sharp and the tall kid called out, 'It's your lucky day, girls, we've come to fuck you hard!' Then the car sped off again while Bea screamed 'Fuck you' and hurled a handful of gravel after it. I froze. I watched the car disappear into the distance while the two boys in the back made crude gestures out of the rear window. I clung onto my bike as my heart pounded and my breathing erupted. Bea turned to me, her face bright-red and her eyes still spitting daggers. She took my bike and laid it gently on the verge. Then she led me up a side lane where we found a grassy bank to sit on. We sat there a long time and she held my hand as I hyperventilated and shook.

'You're alright,' she said. 'No-one's going to hurt you. Just take your time and breathe.'

Gradually, my breathing slowed and the shaking eased off. 'I'm sorry,' I said. 'I feel really stupid.'

'Don't be sorry for something that's not your fault,' said Bea, firmly. 'It's those bastards that should be sorry.'

'Why do they do that?' I asked. 'Why do they think it's okay?'

Bea sighed. 'I don't know. Maybe they've got chromosome envy.'

'Chromosome envy,' I echoed. 'What do you mean?'

'We have two long, elegant X chromosomes,' Bea explained. 'They have one X chromosome and a stumpy, little Y one with hardly any genes on it. It means they're fundamentally unbalanced. Either that or their shared brain cell is having a day off.'

After that, we stayed on site in the afternoons and spent our time paddling in the lake or sunbathing on the front lawn and watching the clouds go by. We discovered we were from the same town and lived only a short bus ride apart. Even better, neither of us was in school so we were going to be able to keep hanging out like that. Technically, we were supposed to be at school but we were both 'school refusers.'

Bea told me that she'd been in care most of her life and, now that she was older, she was living in a house with one other girl and they had a rota of support workers coming in to keep an eye on them. It seemed like she'd moved families and children's homes so often she couldn't even remember them all and, every time she'd moved, she'd had to change school too.

'I soon realised there wasn't much point in going to school,' she said. 'They always put me in the classes for kids who'd given up on learning and with teachers who'd given up on the kids.'

'I don't understand,' I said. 'I haven't known you long but I can see you know as much as anyone I ever met.'

'The secret to a good education,' she confided, 'is to hide in corners in libraries all through the winter. You can read about anything you want and no-one's allowed to interrupt you. The librarians don't mind you being there, as long as you're quiet and don't cause them any trouble. And besides, all the best people were self-taught. Just look at Frida Kahlo.'

I was trying to decide whether or not I should admit that I didn't have a clue who Frida Kahlo was, when Bea continued, 'Then I got my other kind of learning from meeting so many other kids in care. I've pretty much got a degree in all things fucked up. What about you? Did school ever work for you?'

'Mostly it did,' I replied. 'I've had bad days, of course, but mostly I liked it. I've not been able to face it for a few months now, though. Just the idea of it makes me want to curl up or crawl in a hole.'

She didn't ask me why. She just said she was really happy that we were going to be able to keep spending time together.

HOME

As soon as I got home, we went back into lockdown again. To be honest, it didn't really affect me and mum too much. I hadn't been going to school, or anywhere else, for months and mum was spending far too many hours doing agency care work to have time for much else in her life, anyway. Before the virus hit, she'd worked for a big travel agent for years but she was one of the people her firm had let go, right at the beginning. They'd had a big staff Zoom call, one day, and mum and all her colleagues got split up into two smaller groups and mum was in the 'bad luck, you lost your job group,' and that was it.

At first, she was afraid she wouldn't get another job but then she got this agency job and she didn't mind it, except that she had to work all different crazy hours, including nights sometimes. That really sucked for both of us. I hated being in the house on my own all night and mum hated leaving me. She just didn't have any choice 'in the current climate.' When she did have to work a night shift, I often stayed up all night binge-watching comfort-telly like *Friends* so that I wouldn't fall into being scared. Then when mum got home, early in the morning, we'd both go to bed and try and catch up on our sleep.

Things would have been better if dad helped out more but since he did his disappearing act a couple of years ago, with some woman he met at a conference, he'd gotten worse and worse. He'd never been great but I didn't think he'd be the kind of dad that wouldn't hardly bother to stay in touch, but it turned out that was exactly the kind of dad he was. He'd never been one to spend huge amounts of time with me. In fact, looking back, I realise that what he liked best was talking to other people about what a great dad he was and about all the father-daughter things we were going to do together. When it came to it, he didn't really want to do those things at all. He was a talker, not a doer. I try not to think about him anymore but sometimes, when my mind wanders in his direction, I wonder if he still talks about me like that or if he even remembers that he has a daughter at all.

Mum didn't actually ask me if I'd done the counselling at the Starting Over Week. She seemed to assume that I had and there wasn't any point in telling her any different. I'd come back feeling a bit better in myself, anyway, and she was really happy about that. She didn't really mind about the hows and the whys. She tried talking about school and the possibility of me going back but that absolutely wasn't an option in my mind, especially now I had the possibility of hanging out with Bea instead. I was feeling more positive about learning, though. When I first quit going to school, my teachers had sent work home for me but I'd never made more than half-arsed attempts at it and that had petered out. I wasn't even sure if I was still on the school books anymore. I liked Bea's idea of being self-taught though and, since the library was closed, I decided I was going to watch documentaries until I could name famous people that Bea had never heard of. That made mum really happy. She was delighted to see me watching *Into the Inferno* and attempting to sit through *World War II in Colour*.

Mum looking more like herself was a relief to me. She'd had her fair share of dementor days in the last few months, as well. She hadn't been sleeping any better than I had and she'd not been eating properly. Also, she'd come home from work, a couple of times, saying she'd fallen out with people and that wasn't like her. As well as making an effort to learn, I started making more effort around the house. I made sure it was nice and tidy for her every time she got home from work and I picked flowers from the garden to put in a vase on the table, that sort of thing. Bea called round occasionally and we spent the day together. She helped me cook dinner for mum a couple of times but she always left before mum got home. At the time, I thought it was because she wasn't supposed to be there, what with it being lockdown. Later, I realised there was more to it for Bea, though, and she and mum never did meet, which is a shame because I think they would have really liked each other.

That lockdown lasted three weeks. The day we heard it was going to be lifted, Bea came round to make plans with me. She was flushed and excited and chucked a little bag at me as she walked in the door. I followed her into the living room and watched as she threw herself into the patched armchair by the window.

'What's this?' I asked, waving the bag at her.

14

'Take a look,' she replied.

I stuck my hand in the bag and retrieved two small phones. I looked at them, puzzled.

'We've already got phones and these look really basic. What are they for?'

'I got them off a kid I know,' she explained. 'They're going to be our burner phones.'

'Burner phones? What do we need them for? We're not in *Pretty Little Liars.*'

She grinned and leaned forward, eyes shining. 'Lockdown is over and I have a plan hatching in my head and we're going to need these for it. From now on, we only communicate on these phones and no names. No As or Beas or anything else.'

I stared at her, quizzically. Why the melodrama? Surely, she was joking, but she stared right back at me, looking more intense than ever.

IKEA

The first part of Bea's plan involved us meeting up in Bridge Street the next time that mum worked an all-nighter. Bea had been acting really mysteriously and I couldn't begin to guess what she had up her sleeve. The only thing I knew for definite was that she was the best thing that had happened to me in a long time and I was really grateful to be feeling halfway-happy again.

We were supposed to meet at seven but I was a little late because my bus got stuck in traffic. When I finally got there, she was standing outside Boots waiting for me impatiently and hopping up and down with a rucksack on her back.

'Was I supposed to bring anything?' I asked her, once we'd greeted each other.

'No, no, I've got everything we need,' she assured me. 'Follow me.'

We walked down Bridge Street to The Square and headed right, up St. John's Road. The road was named after the church at its far end but these days the church lived in the shadow of the enormous blue and yellow Ikea building next door. That seemed to be where we were heading.

'What time is it?' asked Bea, as we reached the main entrance.

'7.40,' I answered.

'Okay,' she said. 'Let's do this. We haven't got much time.'

We put on our face masks and entered the shop. We went up the stairs and then followed the arrows through the different departments and, as we walked, I could see that Bea's eyes were darting all over the place, looking for something in particular. When we got beyond the large furniture sections, she tapped my arm and we doubled back. Not long after, a bell chimed throughout the store and Bea pulled me into a quiet alcove and whispered, 'Where do you want to hide, the toilets or under a bed?'

'What are you talking about?' I exclaimed.

'We're going to hide and we've only got a couple of minutes to decide where. Toilets or bed?' she repeated.

There seemed no point in arguing, even if I wanted to. 'Bed,' I guess,' I replied.

'Me too, come on,' she hissed.

Quickly, we made our way back to the bedding section which

appeared to be empty.

'That one,' said Bea, pointing at a large bed that was covered with a huge chequered bedspread. Furtively, we walked to the far side of it and dropped to the floor. I scrambled underneath it as Bea pushed at me and her bag, and then pulled herself under as well. It was gloomy under there but I could just make out Bea's features as we removed our face masks. She put her fingers to her lips and raised her head and looked all around to make sure we were completely hidden from view. We lay there for a while, ears pricked and listening intently. Soon we heard heavy footsteps coming from the far end of the hall. I could feel Bea's presence, seemingly calm beside me, but I pulled my fists up to my mouth, tensed my whole body and tried to concentrate on breathing slowly and quietly. There was only one set of footsteps but the owner of them was talking to someone. He was on his phone.

'I've just got to do the rounds a couple of times and make sure all the doors are secure and then I can leave,' he was saying. 'I'll be home really soon.'

There was a pause and then, 'No, I haven't forgotten you're going out. I won't be late. I promise.'

He walked right past the bed and through to the next section. I looked at Bea who put one finger to her lips and kept flashing her other fingers at me. I guessed she meant we had to keep silent for a while longer so I lay there quietly, all the time wondering what the hell she was getting me into.

After a while, the security guard came back. This time he was whistling to himself and he walked straight on through again, which was just as well because if he'd paused or bent down to tie his shoe or done anything suspenseful at all, I'm sure my heart would have burst.

We lay there another ten or fifteen minutes before Bea finally said it was safe to move. Slowly, we rolled out from under the bed. The glare of the main store lights was gone. Instead, a softer glow came from some strip lights on the side walls. They buzzed unobtrusively and two small red lights flashed rhythmically above the lifts. I stood up and stretched as Bea put her rucksack on her back and perched on the side of the bed.

'I feel like you've done this before,' I said.

'Once or twice,' she grinned. 'It's never straightforward, though, because they're always moving things around.'

'And why are we doing it?' I asked.

'Because it's fun,' she replied, 'and when I look at you, I see someone who needs more fun in their life. Am I right?'

I nodded, ruefully.

She jumped up from the blue and yellow bedspread. 'It's time to choose a living room for the evening. Which one do you fancy?'

We headed for the living areas and scrutinized them carefully. 'So,' asked Bea, 'how are you feeling tonight? Shall we go for the sophisticated cream and beige, the jungle green, cosy ochre or how about garish retro?'

'I think,' I said, slowly, 'that the first one is too boring and perfect and the retro one looks too much like vomit. The jungle green is nice and peaceful because of the plants and the wicker but I prefer the ochre red. That sofa looks easily the most comfortable.'

'That would be my choice too,' said Bea. 'As well as being the cosiest it also has the darkest colours. We won't have to worry so much about making a mess.'

'It's got the biggest TV too,' I pointed out.

'True,' said Bea, removing her rucksack and throwing it onto the sofa, 'although we'll have to be our own shows.' She stood in front of the huge screen and did a little jig. I picked up the remote control and waved it at her. She stood to one side of the screen and pointed at it saying, 'This band of pressure here means …'

I laughed and waved the remote at her again. She went back to dancing and then danced off down the hall. 'Come on,' she called back at me as she disappeared around the corner. 'It's Hide and Seek time.'

I raced after her. The next section was kitchens but I could see no sign of her when I got there. I tried to look around systematically, under the tables and in the larger cupboards, but Ikea is not on the side of the seeker. I looked everywhere, with no luck, and then I heard a giggle and footsteps racing away from me.

Next was rugs and, step by step, I went all around the room peering into every crevice I could find. I was looking behind a huge roll of mustard carpet when I suddenly heard an almighty thud. Startled, I jumped back and stared at the large turquoise rug that had appeared on the floor behind me and was now unwinding in my direction. A laughing Bea rolled right out of it and halted at my feet. I helped her up.

'What are you trying to do to me?' I protested. 'That was terrifying.'

'I'm sorry,' she said, 'I couldn't resist it. I wish I could have seen your face when I landed.'

I pulled a panicky Scream face at her and she giggled again as we rolled the carpet up as tightly as we could, put it back on the table she'd rolled it off and headed on.

A large dolls house dominated the next area. Bea headed straight for it, opened it up and started rearranging its inhabitants. 'This house is breaking all the rules,' she said, half to herself. 'There's more than six people in it and they don't seem to have any hand sanitiser.' She lined up the seven small dolls – mum, dad, a girl, a boy, a grandma and grandpa and a baby. She put the mum and the girl on the sofa in front of the telly, she put grandma, grandpa, the boy and the baby in their beds, she

21

put the dad head-first in the kitchen bin and then she jumped up and firmly shut the front of the house.

I was taken aback but saying something didn't seem like a good idea, so I found an arrow to follow and walked on through. We made our way past the mirrors and pictures and then we reached the kitchen utensils area, where Bea stopped again.

'We need stuff to eat and drink from. How about this?' She picked up some plastic plates and cups.

'Are we allowed?' I asked. 'Surely, Ikea won't be happy about us using that stuff?'

'Well, when I invited Mr and Mrs Ikea to this party,' said Bea, 'they said they were very sorry they were unable to join us but we were to be sure to go ahead and use anything we wanted.'

I looked at her, doubtfully.

'We're going to clean them and bring them back after. Stop worrying. If we get caught now, who's going to be worried that we used a couple of unbreakable plates? Come on.'

She pushed the plates and cups into my hands, saying, 'You hold these. I'm getting the Giant Jenga.' Then she picked up a large green bag from a nearby pallet and hugged it to her chest.

ANGRY CONKERS

Back at Cosy Ochre, Bea dragged the beech coffee table out of the way while I opened up the Jenga bag and started setting it up. It took a while and, by the time I'd finished, it was as tall as the telly. I looked round and found that the coffee table was transformed. Bea had covered it with an animal print scarf and filled the plates with crisps and grapes and sandwiches. Two bottles of fruit cider stood expectantly by the cups.

'That looks great,' I said, and looked at Bea. 'You're a terrifying person to hang out with, you know, but you're pretty damn awesome too.'

'Thanks,' smiled Bea. 'You too, although your tower looks kind of cronky. You ready to play?'

We spent the next hour eating and drinking and building and collapsing towers. Once we'd eaten all the food and we'd had enough of construction, we packed up the Jenga blocks, cleaned the plates and cups in the toilets and Bea stuffed the crumby scarf and empty cider bottles back into her bag. We walked the length of the store again, to return everything, and then sprinted back.

Sitting on the carpet, in front of the huge TV screen, Bea revealed her next surprise.

'Have you ever played Angry Conkers?' she asked.

'I've never played any kind of conkers,' I said. 'I've only ever seen conkers played in old movies.'

'That is a tragedy,' declared Bea, gravely, 'but, luckily for you, not an irredeemable one.'

She took four conkers from the front pocket of her bag and gave me two. Each was attached to a foot-long piece of string that was tightly knotted at one end. Bea got me to hold the end of one string and dangle the conker while she demonstrated how to fire the attacking conker.

We had a couple of practices each and then it was time for Angry Conkers.

'I had a really nice foster family once and the kids taught me this game. They used to play it when they were mad at their parents,' Bea explained.

'What happened to the family?' I ventured. 'Why did you leave them?'

Bea looked at me keenly. 'I was afraid the social workers were going to make me see someone I didn't want to see,' she said, 'so I kept running away and, in the end, the foster parents decided I was too much for them.'

'I'm sorry,' I said.

'It's hardly your fault,' she replied.

Bea went first. She had a little rant about lockdown and then drew her conker back and let it fly. It made a resounding crack as it hit my conker square on and sent it soaring straight out of my hand.

My turn. I started with Georgia Dunn who spread rumours about me having nits when we were in Year 7. My conker didn't make quite as good contact as Bea's had but, still, it felt good. After that, I went through Mr Brewer (for shouting at me when I wasn't the one who'd thrown paper balls at him while he'd been writing on the board), the unknown person who'd run my cat over and not stopped, Mimi Bowers (for inviting everyone except me to her birthday party, two years in a row) and loads more.

I was feeling good, really good but, even so, I was shocked to the core when I heard myself say, 'Brett Selby.' Immediately, I froze and a sensation of horror tore through me.

'Go for it,' Bea said, softly.

So, I did. I really went for it but my hand was shaking so much that I missed by miles and my furious conker smashed into the knuckles of Bea's left hand. She didn't make a sound, just dropped her conker and cradled that hand in the other.

'Is he the boy that raped you?' she asked.

'Yeah,' I said.

We sat there quietly for a while and I knew this was an opportunity to talk about what happened but I didn't want it. Then Bea said, 'And did you go to the police?'

'Yes,' I said, staring intently at my conker.

'And do you want to Angry Conker on them?' she asked.

I looked up at her. 'You know everything, don't you?' I said.

'What were their names?' she asked.

'Rachel and Glen, but I feel bad. They were so nice to start with.'

'But?' said Bea.

'But I'm mad at them too.'

'Then go for it,' said Bea. She looked all around. 'It's only me and you here. I'm not going to share this with anyone.' She gave me one of her looks.

'What happens in Angry Conker Club stays in Angry Conker Club. Go for it!'

So, I did. 'This is for Rachel,' I said, 'because when she took my phone, I thought she said they would only look at my messages with Brett but they looked at more than that.'

'That's shit,' said Bea.

'That is shit,' I echoed, as I let my conker go. Crack!

'And what about Glen?' asked Bea.

'Glen,' I said, thoughtfully. 'Well, Glen came to visit me the day before my interview. He was really nice and he chatted about anything and everything and explained what was going to happen the next day. Then, mum and I met him at this special hidden-away building the next morning and he showed us all around. He showed us the waiting room with the little sofas and tables and a pile of the saddest toys you ever saw, all stacked up in the corner. He showed us the interview room with its choice of sofas and huge cameras pointing at every one of them. Then he showed us the recording room next door where Rachel was going to be watching everything. Just inside the door, there were shelves full of blank tapes and DVDs just waiting to be filled with terrible things that hadn't even happened yet.' I paused for breath.

'Which part of that do you want to Angry Conker on?' asked Bea.

'None of that.' I shook my head. 'What I'm mad about is what they didn't tell me and what happened after. I did the interview and it took forever and I had to give so much gruesome detail and it was so incredibly embarrassing and, I know Glen did

27

everything he could to make it okay but, it was still such a difficult thing to do. Afterwards, he told me they were going to bring Brett in for questioning and look at his phone too, but they didn't. And that's what I'm really mad about. We didn't hear from them for weeks after that and then, when they did finally come round, they said they'd found something on my phone that would go against me in court so they weren't going to be able to go ahead with the case. And that meant I got raped, I had the most excruciating, gruelling interview ever, I had my phone interrogated and he had fuck-all happen to him.'

My voice was coming out loud and fast now. 'Why didn't they tell me that they investigate all of their victims but they often don't investigate the suspects? When Rachel first came over, she said she couldn't tell me why Brett had been reported to them before but that he had been and he was definitely a boy to avoid. And she also said they were going to take him in and take his phone. Why did they say that when they knew there was a good chance that they wouldn't? If they'd warned me beforehand, I could have pulled out and saved myself all that intrusion.'

'Was it bad, what was on your phone?' asked Bea.

'I don't know,' I told her. 'Brett was this new kid in the year above me at school. He's stupidly hot and I got a huge crush on him and sent loads of messages to my friend Jazz about how much I liked him and how I wanted to be with him and have sex with him.'

'So, they looked at your phone, discovered you're not the Virgin

Bloody Mary and dropped you,' said Bea.

'It also went against me that we started sending messages the night before we met up and most of it was general chat but some of it was him saying he wanted to jump my bones. Then, the next morning, he sent me dick pics and asked for nudes. They said none of that would look good to a jury because they'd think I should have known what he was about. And then the party we met up at was illegal because there were more than six people at it and so I shouldn't have been there in the first place,' I explained.

Bea looked at me quietly and held up her conker. I concentrated hard and smashed it. A crack appeared and a big piece of the skin flew off.

'That's because they don't give you the 101 reasons why they're not going to be able to help you before they start scrutinizing your life,' I said.

'I'm guessing the kind of sex you were talking to your mate about was nothing like what happened,' said Bea.

'I was imagining the kind of sex where the boy really likes you and cares about you. With cushions and candles and consent. Lots of consent. But that's not what happened.'

'Most boys our age have got their brains so addled with porn, they don't even know there is a caring kind of sex,' said Bea.

I nodded and we sat quietly for a while. I could see that Bea's knuckles were red and slightly swollen.

'I'm sorry,' I said, gesticulating at them.

'It doesn't matter,' she said. 'They'll fix in a day or two. I'm just sorry that all that happened to you.'

'Do you know what really gets me?' I asked. She shook her head.

'It's that, when he raped me, I had the most overwhelming sense of powerlessness. It was like I was so unimportant that he could do anything he wanted to me and no-one would care, except me. Then, when the police first started talking to me, that feeling went away. They made me feel that I was important and that he didn't have the right to do that to me but then, when they said they were dropping the case, that feeling came back worse than ever because then I knew that he could do anything he wanted to me, and there isn't anybody to care about it or do anything about it. And what if it happens again? They're not going to help me, are they? They've already got me down as someone not to be taken seriously.'

Bea moved closer to me and held me tight as I started to cry.

'This can't be right, can it?' I sobbed.

'It's not right,' she said, gravely. 'It's not right at all.'

We sat there a long time while I cried and cried. When I finally stopped, Bea jumped up.

'Don't move,' she said, 'I have an idea.'

She went to the corner of the room and pulled a walking stick from the coat rack on the wall. Then she stood in front of me holding the crook end of the stick. 'Go on one knee for me,' she said. 'I'm the Queen Bee.'

I went on one knee and looked up at her.

Solemnly, she started to speak. 'You have been sorely betrayed by the injustice system of this country and I, therefore, in the name of all that's good and true, proclaim you officially exempt from all the rules of this land, be they sensible or otherwise.' She tapped my shoulders with the stick, 'Arise, Dame Go-Your-Own-Way.'

I rose and headed straight for the bed where I snuggled down under the chequered bedspread. I was shattered after all that emotion. Bea sat on the edge of the bed while I fell asleep. It occurred to me, as I was drifting off, that none of Bea's conker strikes had been about anything personal. It had all been about general things or things that she was angry about for other people. She was an enigma, for sure, but one that I was far too tired to think about right then.

A couple of times in the night, I came to. Bea still wasn't sleeping. First time, she was pacing up and down in front of the lifts and, second time, she was sat on the floor by the bed, singing. I could just see the top of her head. She was singing a song I'd never heard before. It sounded like some kind of lullaby and her voice was surprisingly calm and sweet.

'One evening as the sun went down,
    And sleep to me was calling,
    I fell into a land that's fair and bright,
    Where no-one don't hurt you, day or night,
    Where the lemonade springs,
    And the nightingale sings,
    In the land that's fair and bright.'

OLD FRIENDS

It was around six when Bea prodded me awake.

'Wake up,' she said. 'It's time we got out of here.'

I'd assumed we were going to hide somewhere and then leave the store by the main exit once the doors had opened, but Bea had other ideas.

'I have to get back as soon as I can,' she explained. 'The support worker on at the moment doesn't report me when I go missing, as long as I let her know where I am. The one who's taking over at seven, though, will be straight on to the police if I'm not there and then they'll come looking for me.'

'So, the one who's on at the moment, she knows we're in Ikea?' I asked sleepily.

'No, she's not that cool. She knows I'm with you but she thinks we're at your house and I'm keeping you company while your mum's working nights,' she said.

'That's mostly right,' I said.

'Exactly.'

I got up and we tidied up the bed and then I followed Bea to the nearest stairwell. I was puzzled when we started going up the stairs instead of down.

'Does this mean you've got a getaway helicopter waiting for us on the roof?' I asked.

She laughed. 'I did have one booked but it broke a blade on take-off and the getaway cars are all busy. It's just us and our getaway legs for now.'

On the next level, we walked along a passageway and then we stopped at an emergency exit door overlooking the back car park. Outside the door was a narrow, pitted metal staircase.

'Once we open this door an alarm is going to go off, so we've got to be quick. We've got to get down these steps and over the wall into the churchyard. See those bushes over there, on the far side?' Bea pointed. 'Behind them is another wall which will get us into the back alley behind the church. You should go first. Are you ready?'

I nodded as my heart began to race. I was trying not to think about what mum would say if we got caught. Bea pushed at the emergency bar, said 'NOW' and threw it open. An alarm bell erupted as I ran out, grabbed the rusting stair-rail and headed down as fast as my legs would take me. I was aware of Bea pushing the door closed behind us and then she followed me down.

'Keep going,' she called, as I jumped the last steps to the ground. I raced across the car park, stuck a foot in a crack in the wall and hauled myself over. Once in the cemetery, I ran towards the far corner and the bushes. I looked back and saw that Bea was doubled up with her hand on one of the gravestones.

'Are you alright?' I asked, alarmed.

'Of course, I am,' she grinned at me. 'Come on, we've got this.'

Once we were both behind the bushes, I started to believe that her plan was going to work, we were going to get away. Bea caught up with me at the back wall and gave me a leg-up. I climbed up onto the wall and dropped to the ground the other side. She joined me and we followed the alleyway to the nearest road and then headed away from Ikea. Apart from a light turning on in an upstairs room of one of the terraced houses, all was quiet and peaceful. When we reached the end of the road, Bea suggested we split up. I promised I'd message her to let her know that I'd got back okay and then we hugged and I started on my long trek home.

As it happened, I forgot all about messaging Bea because, when I finally got back, I discovered that mum had been sent home early from work. She'd had a coughing fit after drinking her tea too fast and the man she was working with was worried that it meant she had the virus. She'd tried to explain but he wasn't taking any chances and, so, home she went. She'd arrived back at five, discovered that I wasn't in my bed, found my phone on the table and gone into full on panic. She'd called my old friends Jazz and Andy who, despite me airing them for the last few months, had got themselves out of bed and gone out searching for me. I was really touched when I heard that. I knew I'd been neglecting them and them still being there for me, when they thought I needed them, was probably more than I deserved.

I gave mum a big hug and said I was really sorry but I hadn't been able to sleep so I'd gone for a walk. I felt bad lying about it, especially as she already felt guilty enough that she had to leave me alone some nights. As she bear-hugged me back, I suggested we invite Jazz and Andy over for breakfast and a morning 'sleepover.' That cheered her up. Jazz and Andy had been my closest friends since primary school and they'd slept over at ours, dozens of times. When I'd first stopped going to school, mum had tried to persuade me to invite them over but I hadn't wanted to see anybody, not even them. Once she'd even invited Jazz over herself but I'd assured her that if Jazz came, I was going to shut myself in my room and stay there and if she didn't want to be embarrassed, she should cancel the invite. So, me finally showing some signs of sociability was guaranteed to reassure mum and help her forget my disappearing act.

Mum called them while I dragged the sleeping mats and spare bedding to the living room and set up *The Greatest Showman*. Then I joined mum in the kitchen where we made fruit salad and put chocolate croissants in the oven. It wasn't long before they arrived. Andy came in first and I didn't feel at all awkward with him. He was always so straightforward and smiley and enthusiastic and he was very happy to see that we were ready for the classic sleepover. It was a little harder with Jazz, though. She seemed to be feeling as wary of me as I was of her. We hugged quickly and I mumbled something about being sorry for everything. 'Me too,' she said, which didn't surprise me. I figured she was feeling bad and confused about everything as well, even if she didn't know for sure what had happened.

The week that it happened, Andy had been away with his friend, Yannick. Jazz was around, though, and we'd both been invited to the party although Jazz wasn't allowed to go. Her parents had wanted to know all about it and if it broke the virus rules which, of course, it did because a party with six or less people isn't much of a party. I'd gone round to her house to get ready, though, and she'd done my make-up for me and she'd helped me try out lots of different outfits. She had a particularly short, black skirt that she thought I should wear. When I protested, she pointed out that Maya and Tilly were going to be there and if I wanted to get Brett's attention with them around, I was going to have to play hard-ball. I didn't wear that skirt in the end. I didn't feel comfortable in it, so at least that's one thing no-one can blame me for.

The day after the party, I hadn't wanted to talk to anyone, not even Jazz. She sent loads of messages asking how the party had been and how it had gone with Brett. I aired every one of them and I kept airing her for weeks until, at last, she gave up. She must have worked it out, though. Why else would your best friend from forever go AWOL the night after what was supposed to be the most exciting night of her life?

The 'sleepover' that morning was fun, at least most of the time it was. Meeting Bea seemed to have jolted me into some kind of normality and spending time with Jazz and Andy, watching the things we always used to watch and eating the things we always used to eat, felt good. Maybe, I hadn't lost myself completely. We watched the movie, played some card games and then started watching TikTok videos. We watched cute animals and makeovers and quarantine videos and then we started on funny military voiceovers and they were really funny until Andy said, 'Oh, this reminds me. You know that guy, Brett, that you used to crush on? Apparently, he joined the army in the summer.'

Jazz had my back. I saw her notice the flush that shot up my cheeks. She said nothing to me but managed to distract Andy by getting him to go back to the contouring video. 'Can you do that for me?' she asked him. I was grateful for the excuse to leave the room and get my make-up bag and Andy was reliably glad of the excuse to give someone a makeover. I tried my best to put Brett to the back of my mind for the rest of their stay. I was relieved, though, when Andy got a message from Yannick, reminding him that they were supposed to be going on an XR protest that afternoon. Jazz had agreed to go with them as well, so we all said our goodbyes and they seemed really happy when I agreed to do it all over again the following week.

Once they'd gone, I crashed on my bed and let my thoughts run riot. After a while, I took out my burner phone and messaged Bea what I'd heard. She messaged straight back, 'Glad to hear you got home okay. Weird news. That's one soldier who'll never be a hero. Suppose the good thing is he's out of the way and he might not come back.'

I was still reading her first message when the second one pinged through, 'Does this mean you're friends with al-quaeda now?'

WITHHELD NUMBER

It was late afternoon and I was tidying up, when mum's phone buzzed. I picked it up and took it to her room where she was dozing.

'It says 'withheld number.' Does that mean ...?'

'Probably,' she replied. 'Do you want to talk to them?'

'No,' I said, hurriedly. 'I don't.'

I left the room, shut the bedroom door and sat down on the passage floor.

I traced my finger back and forth along the stripes in the carpet as I listened to mum's end of the conversation. 'Yes,' she said, 'I see, okay.'

That went on for a while and then mum suddenly said, 'Can I ask you something? Would you ever treat a woman the way that boy treated my daughter?'

There was the briefest of pauses and then she said, 'And why not?'

When she spoke again, her voice was rapid and brittle and I couldn't make out the individual words. I gave up. I tipped my head back against the wall and waited for her to finish her conversation and come and find me. Eventually, she said 'goodbye' and then I heard her get up slowly from the creaking bed. She opened the door and called for me.

'I'm just here, mum,' I called up to her. 'What happened?'

Quietly, she pulled me up to my feet and led me to the living room. She sat down on the sofa and patted the seat next to her.

'So?' I asked, as I joined her.

'It's nothing we don't know already,' she sighed.

'Have they talked to him?' I asked.

'Yes, finally.'

'And what happened?'

'They told him you'd made an allegation against him. He said that you'd consented, they told him to be careful in future and I'm afraid that's it, love,' she said.

'That's it?'

41

'That's it.'

'I assume that was Glen you were talking to,' I said.

'Yes.'

'Why did you ask him if he would treat anyone like that? That was a bit weird.'

'I just wanted to make a point. All their focus is about what's going to get past the CPS or a jury and they seem to forget what it's really about.'

'And what's it really about?' I asked her.

'It's about right and wrong and how one human being should treat another. This culture is getting more toxic and dangerous every day. I've been reading about how porn is teaching boys that being manly means being sexually aggressive and about how easy it is for predatory boys to trawl social media sussing out potential victims. Then when they do find vulnerable girls and attack them, the police are so worried about having a case that will stand up in court, they don't deal with the actual problem. If they'd interviewed Brett the first time someone reported him, maybe he wouldn't have gone on to hurt you. Sorry love,' she sighed, pushing a strand of hair out of my face, 'this probably isn't helping you, is it?'

'I don't know,' I shrugged. 'I wonder about that too, what would have happened if they'd talked to him before? Would it have been enough to stop him? It might have been, mightn't it?'

'It might well have been,' she said, 'but I guess they don't get measured on how many crimes they prevent.'

She stood up and walked across to the drinks cabinet.

'Andy said Brett's joined the army,' I told her, as she poured herself a glass of brandy.

Mum nodded. 'Glen said that too. Apparently, they had to go to Collington Barracks to talk to him. Do you want a brandy?' she asked.

'You don't normally let me. Are we having some kind of anti-celebration?'

'Something like that.'

'I guess I'll have one then,' I said.

She poured my drink, put the lid back on the bottle and then handed me my glass as she sat back down. I took a sip and felt the soothing burn of it as it slid down the back of my throat.

We sat staring at the wall, sipping our brandies and then she asked, 'Do you wish we hadn't gone to the police?'

'Yes,' I said. 'It seemed helpful for a while but then it just felt even worse.'

'I'm sorry,' she said. 'You know, when you first told me what happened all I wanted to do was run him over, but I knew that me doing something that drastic wasn't going to help you at all. Going to the police seemed like the only constructive thing we could do. I didn't know that they would just put us on a conveyor belt to nowhere.'

She looked at me sadly, 'Maybe we should have told your dad instead.'

'I told you, I don't want him to know,' I said.

'He could have got a couple of mates together and gone and sorted that boy out. At least, then, there would have been some consequence for him.'

'Dad would have talked a lot about what he was going to do and then he would have done nothing, just like always. The last thing I need is someone else telling me what they're going to do and then not doing it. He's a crap dad and he's full of shit.' My voice accelerated and then I gasped for breath as I finished talking.

Mum stared at me, with a look of astonishment.

'What?' I asked.

'That's the first time I've heard you sounding angry. I think that's a good sign,' she said.

'It's a good sign that I'm badmouthing dad,' I asked.

'Well, you're not saying anything he doesn't deserve,' she said, 'and it's good that you're feeling angry. Up to now, you've been so sad and turned in on yourself but feeling indignant is a good thing. It helps you stand up for yourself.'

I considered telling her about Angry Conkers but that might have led to the whole Ikea story and I wasn't sure if that escapade would have counted as standing up for myself.

'I do feel angry sometimes,' I said. 'I just don't talk about it.'

'And which do you prefer, sad or angry?'

'Do I get any other options?' I asked.

She grimaced and shook her head.

'Do you remember when I was in primary school and I went in for the Xmas poetry competition?'

'Yes, I do,' she said, smiling in recognition.

'I worked really hard at that poem and I was really, really pleased with it and I was so confident that I was going to win. Then they announced that Heidi Jones and I were both disqualified because we'd entered exactly the same poem and they didn't know which one of us had copied the other,' I said.

'But she'd copied you,' said mum, 'and you were fuming because she copied you and because she wouldn't tell the truth and she let you get disqualified.'

'Yes, so then I spent weeks and weeks writing different poems for the Easter competition and when Easter came, I chose my best one and I put it inside three different envelopes and you helped me melt a wax seal on the last one and then I handed it to the teacher and told her not to let anyone go near it, except the judges,' I continued.

'And then when they came to judge it, not only did you win the competition, but they looked at your style of writing and told you that they believed you now, because they could tell that the Xmas poem and the Easter poem were written by the same person.'

'Exactly,' I said, 'and all the time that I was writing those Easter poems, the anger felt like a fire burning inside me and that was great because I could do something with it and turn it into something positive.'

'So, you prefer anger?' mum asked.

'I prefer that anger,' I clarified, 'but this anger is completely different. It's overwhelming. Everything is so big. I can't do anything about any of it and I feel like an animal stuck in a cage, full of rage because it's being treated cruelly and because it's got no control over anything. Compared to this, being sad is easy. All I have to do with sad is close down and let the world go on without me. It's awful and it's miserable but at least I'm not burning up with feelings that I don't know what to do with.'

Mum got the brandy bottle and topped up her glass. 'What about you?' I asked, 'How have you been feeling?'

'Me? I've been feeling furious for so long I'm not sure I remember what it's like to feel anything else,' she said. She reached behind her back, retrieved a cushion and handed it to me. 'Fancy letting out some anger?'

'You know that's the single lamest thing that anyone ever thought of,' I said. 'Who ever got rid of any anger by punching a stupid cushion?'

'I know but I don't know what else to suggest,' she said, 'unless you want to do karaoke? We haven't done that for ages. That's got to be good for excess energy, hasn't it?'

'Seriously?' I said, unconvinced.

'What else are we going to do, apart from drink too much brandy? We could at least try,' she pleaded.

'Okay,' I conceded, grudgingly. 'I'll set it up. What do you want to sing?'

'We could start with *True Colours*,' she said, hopefully.

'Mum, we have sung that song to death!' I protested.

'How about, 'I had breakfast in Texas and lunch in Tennessee,'' she sang.

'And if you start on the country already, I'm going to have to song-bomb you,' I threatened.

'Okay, then, you let me sing *Read All About It* and then you can choose everything else,' she said. 'Final offer.'

I agreed and we sang and it didn't change anything or make anything alright. It didn't stop the fact that Brett had got away with what he did to me and that countless other boys were getting away with it too. What it did do was take the edge off it for a while and, right then, that counted for something.

DONNA

Mum took the next couple of days off work so it was a while before I was free to meet up with Bea again. As soon as mum left, I messaged to tell her the coast was clear and was surprised when she called me straight back and invited me to her place.

'I didn't think you were allowed visitors,' I said.

'We're not, but sometimes we sneak people in,' she replied.

'And how does that work?' I asked.

'Planning, synchronisation and deception. Do you know the corner shop at the top of Lime Hill?'

'I think so,' I said.

'Can you be there in an hour's time and, when you get there, call me and I'll tell you what to do next,' she instructed.

'Nothing is ever straightforward with you, is it?'

'I didn't choose this life,' she protested. 'I'd love to live somewhere where my friends could just come to the door and I could let them in, but that's not how it is. Can you make it in an hour?'

'Yeah, I'll be there. See you soon.'

I arrived a little early at the corner shop. I browsed the brightly-coloured, cluttered shelves and bought some snacks. Then I went outside and found a quiet spot from which to phone Bea.

'It's me,' I told her, as she picked up.

'Good,' she said. 'Now you just have to walk a little way down Lime Hill and turn left, just before the bus stop, into Waterhouse Lane. We're half-way down on the left. Number 17. I'll leave the door open for you. Go straight upstairs and mine's the first bedroom on the left. Go in there and wait for me and be really quiet.'

'Where are you going to be?' I asked.

'I'm going to the shops with Jen, the support worker, to get her out of the way. We'll pass you and you'll have to pretend you don't know me. The other girl in the house, Donna, is still sleeping. It's not the end of the world if she wakes up and sees you, but if you can try and be quiet and invisible that might be best,' she said.

'Okay,' I agreed. 'I'll see you in a bit.'

I set off down Lime Hill, dodging a skate boarder, who seemed intent on running me over, and a couple of kids on bikes. As I rounded the corner into Waterhouse Lane, I saw Bea and a short, squat, blonde woman coming towards me. I walked past them with my eyes fixed firmly ahead and my ears bending in their direction.

'Haven't you been to the shop today, already?' Jen was saying, crossly, to Bea. 'Why didn't you buy shampoo then?'

'I'm really sorry. I forgot,' Bea was saying, placatingly.

Poor Bea, I thought. What a palaver.

I found number 17 and, good as her word, Bea had left the door on the latch. I pushed it open, slipped into the house and glanced around. There was a living room on the right and a kitchen straight ahead. The stairs were to the left and I crept up them. I didn't want to frighten Donna. The worn carpet on the stairs absorbed my footsteps and I made it up without a sound. At the top of the stairs, I turned left and found Bea's bedroom door wide open. I entered, shut the door and looked around.

Bea's room was bigger than my bedroom. The bed was underneath a large, sash window and outside was a sparse little garden with a circle of grass and a rowan tree. Inside the room, there was an Ikea wardrobe and a bright green tub chair next to the door. Opposite that was a large, battered desk with two rows of bookshelves above it. The bookshelves were rammed to bursting and the desk was completely covered with

51

drawings. I picked up the top one. It was of a warrior woman sitting on a majestic-looking black horse. The woman herself had a mane of long, red hair, wore a green tunic and carried a decorative bronze shield and a spear that dripped with blood.

I heard the front door swing open and footsteps come bouncing up the stairs. Bea was back. I hid out of sight as she came in, not sure what to expect. 'It's okay,' she said, 'you don't have to hide. Jen's not allowed in here. What have you been doing?'

'Not much,' I said, 'I've not been here that long. I was just looking at these pictures. I didn't know you could draw.'

'I've always loved drawing,' she said. 'Look at these.' She leafed through the piles of pictures, pointing out the ones she was particularly pleased with. They were mostly mythological and fantastical creatures and ancient heroes.

'You're really lucky,' I said. 'I wish I could draw like that.'

'It's just practice,' she said. 'If you do something enough and really think about how you're doing it, you get good at it. Look.' She grabbed an art book from the bookcase and opened it up at a picture of an old man in a three-piece suit sitting on a chair. 'I bet that you could draw this,' she said.

'No way,' I said. 'I couldn't begin to draw that.'

She got me a piece of paper and a pencil and cleared some space on the desk. Then she turned the art book upside down.

'What are you doing?' I protested.

'I'm helping you to see what this picture really looks like so that you can draw it,' she said. 'If you look at it the right way up, it will be familiar to you and your brain will jump to conclusions about how everything fits together and then you'll go wrong. If it's upside down, you have to take the time to look at it properly and to see where the lines really are and how they link up. Try it. I promise you you'll get a better result.'

I sat down and examined the upside-down picture. I measured out the lines, looked carefully at the angles between them and began to replicate them. Bea sat on her bed reading, while I worked. I must have been there almost an hour, drawing and checking and redrawing, before I was happy that I'd got all of the lines from the original picture.

'I'm done,' I finally called out to Bea. 'Do you want to have a look?'

'I do,' said Bea, encouragingly. 'Turn it around.'

So, I turned around my picture and the book and compared them and, although it wasn't brilliant, I had to admit it surpassed any of my previous attempts at art.

'Was I right or was I right?' asked Bea. 'I think it's pretty good.'

'Thanks,' I said, chuffed with both my efforts and her praise.

Bea smiled and then looked pointedly at my bag that I'd

abandoned at the end of her bed. 'I didn't want to disturb you while you were concentrating,' she said, 'but did you bring any snacks?'

'I did,' I said, remembering. 'I got crisps and apple juice in the shop. What about you? Did you get anything apart from shampoo?'

'I didn't,' sighed Bea. 'Jen gets suspicious really easily so I thought I'd better keep it simple. Donna might have some biscuits, though. I could see if she wants to join us, if you don't mind?'

'Sure,' I said. 'I don't mind.'

Bea cut across the landing and dived through the door opposite. At once, there was an almighty scream and I heard Bea exclaim, 'What the hell are you doing? Put some clothes on.' Then there was sobbing and the sound of Bea talking angrily and emphatically.

After a few minutes, Bea returned. She was flushed and agitated. 'Fuck,' she cried, as she strode furiously around the room. 'What is wrong with boys?' I waited for her to continue but before she could there was a cautious knock at the door.

'Come in,' called Bea.

A tiny girl with knotty black hair tip-toed into the room. Her face was a streaky, bronze colour but the limbs that stuck out

54

of her baggy Moana T-shirt were porcelain-pale except for the dark, red lines that she'd carved into them.

'Hi,' she said shyly. Bea introduced us and, in the conversation that followed, I gradually worked out what had happened. A few weeks earlier, a boy called Brady Dunbar had sent Donna dick pics and asked for nudes. She'd sent them and ever since he'd been blackmailing her for more. She'd been taking some for him when Bea walked in.

'He says I'm a whore for sending pictures in the first place and if I don't send exactly what he wants, then he's going to send them to thousands of people and everyone will know what I'm like,' explained Donna.

'Then tell him you're going to send his dick pics to thousands more,' said Bea, her voice full of frustration.

'It's different for boys, though,' said Donna.

'But why?' cried Bea. 'How many unasked-for nudes have you sent in your life? And how many unsolicited dick pics has that creep sent? It's not right. That kid is an evil, fucking hypocrite. Someone should stop him.'

'But who?' asked Donna. 'There isn't anyone to stop him.'

'Yes, there is,' said Bea, looking first at Donna and then at me. 'There's us. We're going to stop him. We're going to steal his phone and decimate it.'

'But he says he's got images on his laptop as well as his phone. We can't get hold of that. It'll be in his house,' said Donna.

'Then we'll have to find a way to get into his house,' said Bea, simply. 'Won't we?' She looked at me.

'I'd like to help,' I said, nervously, 'but I'm not sure I'm up for breaking and entering.'

Bea laughed. 'How do you think you got in here today or out of Ikea last week? You're a natural at breaking and entering.'

I looked at her, unconvinced.

Bea sighed. 'If we plan it properly and if we can find a way to do it without breaking anything, are you in?'

I hesitated.

'Think about how many other girls that arsehole is doing this to? Somebody has to stop him and you know that if we don't do it, no-one will. Am I right?'

'Okay,' I said. 'You're right. I'm in.'

'Donna?'

'Of course,' she said, 'if you two will, then so will I.' She stood up, grinned at me and leapt onto the bed.

Bea got out a notepad and we sat around making plans.

Donna told us that Brady lived with just his dad and that their house was half-way between Victoria Park and the town centre. She had him on Snap Maps and seemed to be quite an expert on his movements. She knew that, after school every day, he spent two or three hours at the skate park on this side of town and then he went home. Our basic plan was simple. We had to find a time and a way to get into his house and steal his laptop and then, immediately afterwards, we had to steal his phone and smash the both of them to smithereens. Bea drew a map of her house, Brady's house, Victoria Park and the skate park. She tore it out of her notepad and stuck it on the notice board behind the door.

On the next piece of paper, she drew a line across the middle. On the top half of it, she wrote, 'BOYS TO AVOID' and on the bottom half she wrote, 'POSSIBLY OK BOYS.'

'Give me some ideas for crappy boy characteristics,' she said, 'and I'll make a list.' So we did and this is what the list looked like:

1. Sends dick pics
2. Sends animal dick pics
3. Sends wanking videos
4. Asks for nudes
5. Only compliments you on your 'arse' or your 'tits'
6. Never asks how you are or shows any interest in your actual life

Then we made the possibly okay boys list which was kind of an opposites list really:

1. Doesn't send or ask for nudes
2. Shows a genuine interest in you
3. Compliments you on things that aren't about sex
4. Talks about things that aren't sex or weed or mandy

'All you have to do, Donna,' said Bea, 'is stick to boys from the second list. If anyone does anything from the first list, block them straight away.'

'But I don't think I know any boys who'd make it onto the second list,' Donna pointed out.

'Then block them all,' said Bea.

'How am I going to find a boyfriend if I block them all?' wailed Donna.

'What kind of boyfriend do you want?' insisted Bea. 'If you really don't know anyone who'll treat you right, you'll just have to become more independent or gay or patient or something.'

'It's alright for you. You're not into boys,' said Donna.

'Show me a boy who doesn't think with the wrong head and I might be,' retorted Bea.

'Has anyone ever sent you a dick pic?' I asked Bea, thinking they probably hadn't.

'Not many. The ones that have, I messaged them that I'd seen more appealing blobfish and then I blocked them.'

'What's a blobfish?' I asked.

Bea picked up her phone and googled 'blobfish.' The weirdest-looking fish I'd ever seen appeared on the screen.

'Yuck,' said Donna. 'That's gross in a really sad kind of a way.'

'Isn't it?' said Bea. 'It's perfect.'

RECONNAISSANCE

The following afternoon, I met Bea and Donna at the bandstand in Victoria Park. It was a gloomy day and the park was fairly quiet. A homeless man sat on a bench in one corner and there were a few parents with their little kids in the playground. There was no-one near the bandstand at all, just a surrounding circle of rosebushes which was well past its summer splendour.

Donna was looking much more cheerful and was balancing on the wooden railings, attempting to do a complete circuit without falling off. 'Everything is going to be fine,' she told me. 'We're going to teach Brady to be careful who he messes with and then I'm going to find a boyfriend who's not a complete loser.' I looked at Bea quizzically as Donna lost her balance and fell into the rosebushes below. 'Ouch,' she complained, as she landed.

'We went through all her contacts last night and she made the happy discovery that not all the boys she knows are creeps. She's been telling Jen that she doesn't have to put up with anyone treating her badly anymore,' explained Bea.

'That's great,' I said, 'so, now we just have to sort the Brady situation. What's the plan?'

'You and I should go and check out his house now, while he's at school, and see what we can find out and how easy it's going to be to get in there,' said Bea. 'I think Donna should stay here.'

'That's okay with me,' said Donna. 'I don't want to go anywhere near that idiot's house. I'll keep an eye on Snap Maps for you and let you know if he moves.'

Brady's house was a little less than a mile away. It was set back on a downward slope and was surrounded by tall hedges. The house was to the left of the driveway and there was a dark, shady area to the right, next to a shed. We stepped into the shade and Bea took a photo of the house. There were a couple of open windows on the upper floor at the front, but none downstairs. There was also no sign of a security camera anywhere. The front door was to the nearside of the house, next to the driveway. There were a couple of wide steps going up to it and plant pots on either side. Both the pots were home to neatly-trimmed little holly trees.

Bea fiddled with the shed door and prised it open. 'There's a ladder in here if we need it,' she said. 'I wonder if they leave the windows at the back of the house open.' She stepped out of the shade, ran down the driveway and disappeared around the back of the house.

I was thinking about following her when, all of a sudden, a green van sped down the road and pulled into the drive.

Startled, I leapt backwards and hoped and prayed that I hadn't been seen. I stared, mesmerised, as the door of the van slowly opened. The side of the van was emblazoned with the words 'Dunbar Garden Landscaping.' A tall, stocky man in jeans and a check shirt got out of the driver's seat and spotted me immediately.

'Hello,' he said. 'Are you a friend of Brady's?'

'No,' I said, as my heart began to thump.

'Then how can I help you?' he asked, curiously.

'Umm,' I stuttered, 'I was just, umm, looking at those plants by your door. It's my mum's birthday next week and I want to get her something nice and that's just the kind of thing she likes.'

I started to tremble as he walked towards me but he smiled broadly and reassuringly. He took a card from his pocket and handed it to me. 'Take this. If your mum ever needs a gardener, get her to give me a call. I could get a holly tree like that for you at a good rate but it'll still set you back about £20. How much do you love your mum?'

'That's probably a bit much,' I said, 'but I could talk to my mum about it. I'll definitely give her your card. Thanks for your help.'

I put the card in my pocket and left the driveway. I looked back and noticed that Brady's dad was leaning over the farthest plant pot and removing what must have been a key. Bingo! Now all

I needed to do was find Bea.

I messaged her as I walked, 'Where the hell are you? You've got to get out of there.'

'Already did,' she messaged back. 'There's a back gate. What happened to you?'

I told her about my ad-libbing and about the key.

Bea was delighted. 'Didn't I tell you you're a natural at this?' she said. 'Hopefully, we won't need that ladder.'

We messaged each other until our paths crossed further up the road and then we headed back to Donna and the bandstand. We sat on the cold, concrete floor and I handed Brady's dad's business card to Bea.

'Matt Dunbar, Dunbar Garden Landscaping, No Job Too Big or Too Small,' she read. 'This is perfect, now all we have to do is get Matt Dunbar out of the way by asking him to go and do a quote in another town.'

'Merton Newbury's quite far,' said Donna. 'My last foster placement was in a big house out there. They've got a big garden. I could give you their address to use.'

'You could ask him to do a quote for a re-landscaping,' I suggested.

Bea smiled, got out her phone and started typing. 'Hi, my garden in Merton Newbury is a third of an acre and is looking very dull. Would you be able to have a look and give me a quote for a complete garden makeover? Late afternoon is best for me, Tanya.'

While we waited for a response, we talked about the finer details of our plan. We all thought it best if we dressed as boys so, if anything went wrong and anyone did see us, they wouldn't be able to give an accurate description of us to anybody. 'Have you both got roadman clothes you can wear?' asked Donna. 'I've got stuff you can borrow if you haven't.'

'I've got black trackies and a black hoodie,' I said.

'Me too,' said Bea.

'You've got to learn to walk like this,' said Donna. She pushed her trackies half-way down her bum, dropped her left shoulder and sauntered around the bandstand. She pointed gun fingers at me, screwed up her face and said, 'Nah, brudder, I'm not 'aving that, big man ting.'

'I'm sorry, my g,' I said, and threw some hand shapes back at her.

'You my fam, innit?' she said, laughing.

'It's a good job you're going to be back home, manning the phones and Snap Maps,' Bea told her. 'You're funny, but I don't think you're going to fool anybody.'

Just then, Bea's phone buzzed. She looked down and grinned. 'Got him,' she said. 'Matt Dunbar wants to come and do a quote on Friday at 3pm. Give me that address, Donna, and we're all set.'

ANDY

Thursday night was the night Jazz and Andy were due to come round again. Mum's mood visibly lifted when I reminded her. 'What are you all going to do?' she asked. 'Do you want me to help get anything ready or buy anything special?'

'Don't worry,' I told her. 'I'll just cook some pasta or something when they get here and then we'll make it up from there. Andy's got some environmental film he really wants us to watch, apparently. They've got no school tomorrow, it's a teacher training day, so we'll probably be up late.'

'That's okay, I'll just have a good tidy up and then I'll leave you to it,' she said.

I was sitting at the kitchen table, playing games on my phone, when Jazz arrived. Our out-of-tune doorbell did its flat rendition of *Fur Elise* and mum got the door. 'Hi Jazz, it's so lovely to see you,' I heard her say. 'Come on in.'

I looked up as mum brought her through. Jazz smiled, as she put her bag down in the corner, but she looked pale and upset.

'What's wrong,' I asked. 'Has something happened?'

'It's Andy,' she said. 'He and Yannick just got arrested.'

'He what?' gasped mum. 'What can Andy have done that warrants being arrested?'

Jazz came and sat next to me at the table. Mum took the chair opposite and stared fixedly at Jazz. 'What's going on?' she asked. 'What did he do?'

'I don't know much about what's going on now,' said Jazz. 'We went to pick Andy up on the way here but there wasn't anyone in. I knocked a couple of times and I tried calling his phone but there wasn't any answer on that, either. Then I tried his dad and he said that they were all at the police station and that Andy and Yannick had been arrested and they're going to be charged with, let me check.' She looked at her phone and read out the message from Andy's dad. 'They're being charged with trespass and vandalism and displaying a sign intended to cause alarm or distress.'

'Displaying a sign intended to cause alarm or distress?' echoed mum. 'How can that be a crime? What exactly did they do?'

'That I do know because they've been posting pictures of it all day,' explained Jazz. 'Last night they did a mass banner drop. I think they've been planning it for ages. Look, I'll show you.' She got up a video of Andy and Yannick. They were both wearing trackies and XR sweatshirts and brightly-coloured bandanas and they were standing outside the central fire station. It must have been late because, as well as being dark, there wasn't any traffic noise at all.

'They went to the central fire station and climbed up the training tower and dropped this banner from the top.' Jazz pulled up the next video and showed it to us. Yannick was at the top of the tower holding something, then he counted down 3-2-1 and let it drop. A swathe of green and orange fabric appeared, emblazoned with the words, 'THE AMAZON'S BURNING. PUT IT OUT.'

'And that's why they've been arrested,' said mum, incredulous.

'Well, that was just the beginning of it,' explained Jazz. 'Then they went to the fire station on the other side of town and they dropped another banner like that. Then they went up to the airport and hung this up.' She showed us a photo. Andy was standing next to the airport fence and pointing at the large banner that they'd attached to it. On the banner was a picture of a crying earth and it had the caption – 'MeToo, says Mother Earth.'

'And then,' continued Jazz, 'they went into the centre of town, and look.' She pulled up another video. It showed Yannick scurrying up a spiral staircase that, Jazz said, was at the back of the town hall. Andy must have been running up after him with the camera, because the film was really jolty.

'Now watch,' she said. The staircase came to an end at the top of the building and gave on to a door. Yannick reached up the wall, put his foot on the door handle and pushed himself up. The camera jerked upwards and we saw Yannick's hands holding onto the balustrade on the roof of the building. He hung on and walked himself up the wall and over the top. Andy must have followed him because next was a load of selfies of the two of them, set against the views from the top of the building. Finally, there was a picture they'd taken once they'd got back to ground level. It was of a huge banner running across the top of the town hall which declared, 'STOP FIDDLING. THE WORLD'S BURNING.'

'And how do the police know it was them?' asked mum.

'Well, they're not exactly keeping it a secret. They've posted it on every social media platform they can think of. They want people to know about it.'

Mum shook her head. 'How can caring about the planet and protesting peacefully be worth police time, when the police aren't doing anything about really serious crimes?'

'I know,' said Jazz. 'It doesn't make any sense at all.'

Mum put her head in her hands and sighed. 'I can't believe they've been arrested for trying to make the world better,' she said. 'I feel like I should do something to help them but I don't know what. What can I do?'

'I can think of one thing,' said Jazz. 'Andy's always really loved those chocolate flapjacks you make. Why don't you make him some of those and we can take them to him tomorrow? Then at least he'll know you're thinking of him.'

'I was hoping for something a little more dynamic and bold, but I guess he would appreciate flapjacks. How about you two go and buy some oats and chocolate and while you're doing that, I'll make us a lasagne,' suggested mum.

'I was going to cook for us,' I started to say, but Jazz interrupted me. 'That would be really nice,' she said. 'We'll go now.'

'Your mum seems really stressed,' pointed out Jazz, as we walked down the front path, rounded mum's car and crossed the road. 'Is she okay?'

'I don't know. I'm worried about her. There's been a lot going on recently and none of it's been good. I know she's not eating or sleeping properly.'

'It's nice she cares so much about Andy. Do you think she'd care that much if it was me?' asked Jazz.

'Of course she would, she loves you both,' I said.

'She seems desperate for something positive to do.'

'Yeah, I guess she's spent a lot of time feeling powerless recently,' I said, 'and that's a pretty crappy feeling to be stuck with.'

'And what about you?' asked Jazz.

I thought about Bea and Donna and our plan for the next day.

'Do you know, I'm beginning to feel a bit better on that one,' I told her.

By the time we got back, the lasagne was in the oven and starting to smell enticing. Jazz and I laid the table and poured drinks while mum made a salad. Then mum served up and we all sat down and tucked in.

'Your cooking's always so good,' declared Jazz. Mum smiled appreciatively and asked after Jazz's parents. Jazz explained how worried they were about the virus and how her mum was constantly cleaning everything and following everyone in the family around with hand sanitiser. 'I just want it to be over,' said Jazz, 'so that my parents can stop stressing about everything and go back to being normal.'

Once we'd eaten and cleared up, Jazz and I went off to do quizzes and listen to music. It must have been 10.30 before I checked on mum again. She was sat at the table, playing patience, with an almost empty brandy bottle beside her. 'Are you okay, mum?' I asked.

'Did you know,' she said, 'the beauty of a game like patience is that it doesn't matter how many times it goes wrong? Whatever happens, you can always start over again and again until it comes right.'

'Are you drunk?' I asked suspiciously. 'You're slurring your words.'

'Maybe a little, but I don't know what else to do. The world's getting more twisted every day.' She gathered up the playing cards and started to shuffle them haphazardly. 'Andy and his friend didn't even damage anything, did they? If the police can come up with spurious charges like vandalism and putting up alarming signs so that they can arrest them, why can't they do more about boys like Brett? They could have looked at his phone and checked if he'd been watching illegal porn or if he'd been harassing girls online before they decided not to do anything about him. I just can't get my head around how skewed their priorities are. I can't, it doesn't, I ...' She shook her head and sighed as tears started to trickle down her cheeks.

I put my arms around her and hugged her tight.

'I'm sorry,' she said. 'I'm supposed to be strong for you. I shouldn't be doing this.'

'It's okay,' I told her. 'No-one can be strong all the time and, you're right, Andy getting arrested, and Brett not being arrested, completely, completely sucks. It's not fair.'

She took another sip of brandy and gave me a rueful smile.

'Jazz and I are going to watch this film that Andy's been talking about. Why don't you join us?' I asked.

'I don't think so,' she replied. 'I can't concentrate on anything at the moment. My brain won't focus. You watch. I think I should go to bed. Maybe, in the morning, the world might make some sense again.'

'I wouldn't count on that,' I said, 'but at least you might be yourself again.'

I helped her to bed and then Jazz and I stayed up late watching Andy's movie and a load of David Attenborough clips.

I was right about the next morning. Mum was back to being mum. She'd left for work long before we got up and she'd left a tray of flapjacks on the counter with a note. It said, 'Sorry about last night. Made these this morning. Give them to Andy and Yannick and tell them I couldn't be prouder of them. Love you xx'

I was also right about the world. It wasn't making any more sense at all. Jazz and I both woke up to messages from Andy saying that he'd been bailed but they'd put an ankle tag on him and given him a curfew. He wasn't allowed out of his house between 7pm and 7am.

My message from Bea was more encouraging, though. It said, 'D-Day! Ready to take down Brady Dunbar?'

'And some,' I messaged back.

It was a bit tricky trying to explain to Jazz that I wasn't going to be able to go straight round to Andy's with her, without being able to tell her why. 'Trust me, Jazz,' I pleaded. 'I have to do something really important and, most of the time, I'd put Andy first, but today I can't. I'm really, really sorry.'

She looked at me suspiciously. 'You're not in trouble, are you?' she asked.

'Of course not, only good people get in trouble.'

I packed up mum's flapjacks and handed them to Jazz with the note. 'Tell Andy I'll come round as soon as I can. I'll come and brighten up his curfew for him, I promise.'

BRADY

I met Bea at 2.20, in Allenby Road which led into Brady's road. We were both dressed head to toe in black – hoodies, trackies, trainers and face masks, and Bea had her dark-coloured rucksack, stripped of any identifying badges or marks. 'Did you remember the gloves?' she asked.

'Of course,' I said, pulling them out of my pocket. 'Here's mum's extra skinny gloves for you and I've got my normal winter ones.'

'Brady's supposed to be at school but he must be bunking off for the afternoon because Donna says he's been at the skate park since two.'

'And what about his dad? Has he left yet?' I asked.

'The van was still there when I walked past just now.' She craned her neck and said, 'I can just about see the end of their driveway from here, and it's still there.'

I stood restlessly while she peered past my head. 'What if he forgets or doesn't leave the key,' I fretted.

'Then we do it another day,' said Bea. 'Stop worrying and remember …' She smiled. 'Don't look, but he is just pulling out of the driveway and … now, he is driving up the road.'

I managed not to look and we turned and walked up one side of Allenby Road and down the other before we ventured into Brady's road. Then we walked towards his house with our best casual roadman amble. I stopped to look around and Bea headed for the holly trees. 'Coast is completely clear,' I whispered, as I joined her and put on my gloves.

'Help me tip this pot up,' murmured Bea. I did and, as soon as the pot started to tip, we could see the wonderful shape of a shiny Yale key. 'Didn't I promise you no breaking?' said Bea. The relief in her voice was almost tangible.

Quickly, she scooped up the key, jumped up the steps, put the key in the lock, turned it and we were in. It was unbelievably, frighteningly easy!

The house seemed bright and spacious but we didn't stop to look around. We shot upstairs and took half the doors each, just like we'd planned. 'Over here,' called Bea, softly, on her second attempt. I ran across to her. 'This has to be his room. It's all Chelsea posters and video games and there,' she pointed triumphantly, 'is his laptop. You check his drawers and cupboards for any other devices and I'll sort this out.'

There was a tortoiseshell cat curled up on the duvet. It looked up at me, as I bent down to check the large drawers under the bed, and then it rolled over and stretched. I opened the first drawer. 'Ugh,' I exclaimed, 'I've found his smelly trainers' drawer. Wow, that has got to be a biohazard!' I searched amongst his shoes and then looked in the other drawer and the wardrobe. Meanwhile, Bea had removed the cable to the laptop and placed the laptop neatly in her rucksack.

'You found anything else anywhere?' she said.

'Nothing,' I said. 'Can we get out of here now?'

Bea insisted on double-checking all the cupboards. 'Come on, we've got what we need. Let's just go,' I pleaded. Now that I had nothing to do, anxiety was kicking in.

'One more thing,' insisted Bea.

She opened the front pocket of her rucksack and took out a conker on a string. She held it above the space where the laptop had been and lowered it slowly to the desk top. Then she spiralled the string neatly around the nut.

'We're leaving calling cards now?' I said.

'There's nothing wrong with being professional,' she replied.

She stroked the cat and then we ran down the stairs and straight out of the door. Getting caught out by Brady's dad on our previous visit had been useful in more ways than one. Bea showed me how she'd escaped that day. The back gate was a bit stiff but it opened just wide enough for us to squeeze out of the garden and into the overgrown alleyway behind. We ducked down under the overhanging branches and made our way to the road. Once there, we headed in the general direction of the skate park for around a quarter of a mile. Then we found somewhere to sit and message Donna.

'Stage 1 complete,' we wrote. 'Where is he?'

'He just left the skate park,' she messaged back. 'He's heading home. Be quick. He's moving fast.'

'Shit,' said Bea. 'Where can we head him off?'

'Crowley Road,' I suggested.

'I don't think we'll get there in time. What if we miss him? We can't take that chance. Shit, what should we do?'

I looked at her as we both came to the same conclusion. 'We've got to go back the way we came, haven't we?' I said.

'It's the only way to make sure we catch him,' she agreed. 'If we don't get his phone this is all a waste of time. We don't even know if there is anything on the laptop.'

We walked quickly back to the alley, stooped under the trees and went through the back gate. Bea beckoned me to follow her and we positioned ourselves just inside the front garden, behind the hedge. It wasn't long before we heard the rumble of a skateboard. Donna was right. He was moving fast.

'You ready,' whispered Bea. 'Remember, no talking.' I nodded.

As he sped around the corner of the driveway, Bea stepped out in front of him. They both groaned as they collided and the skateboard clattered to one side. Brady went flying onto the front lawn and Bea was thrown back onto the hedge and then she fell awkwardly to the ground. I reached towards her but she waved me away and I remembered what I had to do. I ran towards Brady but then saw that his phone was lying in the grass a few feet away. As I went to grab it, he realised what I was trying to do and hurled himself in front of me. For a moment, I thought I'd messed it all up but then there was an almighty crack and he fell flat to the ground. I looked around, shocked, and saw that Bea had picked up his skateboard and wrapped it around his head. I seized the phone, shoved it in my pocket and we ran and ran and ran.

We didn't stop until we got to Victoria Park. Once we got there, we dived breathlessly into some rhododendron bushes and took off our hoodies and the brightly-coloured tops that we wore underneath them. Then we put them back on, only the other way around. 'I'll message Donna,' said Bea. While she did that, I put Brady's phone in her rucksack with the laptop, and then we waited for Donna to join us.

Back at my house, forty minutes later, the fun bit began. Mum was on a long shift and wasn't due back until late. That meant we had plenty of time to destroy all the pictures that Brady had extorted from Donna and from who knows, who else. We put a blanket on the floor and raided the garage for hammers. 'Anyone want to try and hack into either of these things before we start?' asked Bea.

'I think we've seen enough of Brady Dunbar's soul,' I replied. 'Let's just obliterate it!'

We let Donna have the first blow. Solemnly, Bea handed her the hammer and she let fly at the phone. The screen shattered and a huge dent appeared in the metal beneath. It took longer than we expected, to pulverise both devices, and we couldn't do much with the metal except hammer it out of all recognisable shape. It took a good hour in all, but annihilating Brady Dunbar's sordid life turned out to be one of the most therapeutic hours that any of us had ever spent.

HITCHCOCK

A few days later, mum got called in last minute for a late shift. 'Are you going to be okay if I go?' she asked, with an all-too-familiar worried look on her face. 'I won't be back until midnight, probably.'

'I'll be fine,' I assured her. 'I'll invite someone over.'

'Well, you can't invite Andy. He's not allowed to go anywhere in the evenings, is he?'

'No, and he's really not happy about it. I could ask Jazz, though. Hopefully her parents will let her come.'

'How's Andy doing, anyway?'

'Well, he's getting about four support messages for every bit of hate mail he gets so he's decided that's a positive. What he's really struggling with is not being able to see Yannick. Part of their bail conditions is that they don't see each other, and they've both got tags on so they've got no choice but to stick to it.'

Mum shook her head. 'I feel a rant coming on,' she said. 'Do you want to hear it or shall I just go to work?'

'Just go to work and don't worry about me. I will be fine. I promise.'

As soon as mum's car started up and pulled away, I messaged Bea. 'I'm free for a few hours now. Can you come over?'

She replied immediately. 'Thought you'd never ask. I'm on my way.'

It wasn't long before I heard a determined knocking on the front door. I opened it and Bea burst in, dripping with positivity and purpose. She put a pizza on the kitchen worktop and handed me a DVD.

'What's this?' I looked at the black, red and white cover. A bald man in a suit stood with his hand hovering over a small picture of a train. 'Alfred Hitchcock. *Strangers on a Train*,' I read.

'If you like it, it's a doorway to a world of suspense and thrills,' said Bea, as she took the pizza out of the box and put it on the oven tray. 'And if you don't like it, it's still going to be a doorway. Trust me. Go and put it on.'

Twenty minutes later, we'd made ourselves comfortable with pizza and drinks and Bea started the film. It was slow. I'd never seen a black and white movie before and this one spent the first ten minutes zooming in on black and white shoes and train lines. It got really good, though, once the talking started. The two main characters meet on a train. One of them, Guy, is a famous tennis player and the other one, Bruno, is a psychopathic rich guy. He knows that Guy is trying to get a divorce from his wife and he suggests that they swap murders. Guy's shocked but he humours Bruno who decides to take his response as consent. Soon after, Bruno tracks Guy down, announces that he's killed his wife for him and insists that Guy owes him a murder.

Once it had finished, Bea turned to me expectantly, 'What do you think?'

'It was good. I'd watch another one,' I said.

'But what do you think?' she said, with emphasis. 'Shall we do it?'

'Do what?' I asked, as the hairs began to stand up on the back of my neck.

'Shall we swap murders?' she asked.

'Swap murders,' I squeaked, in an alarmed voice. 'What are you saying? Are you offering to murder Brett?'

'Something like that,' she agreed.

'And what do you want me to do in return?'

She turned on her phone and brought up Facebook. She typed

in 'Dale Tarrant' and a man who resembled a younger version of Alfred Hitchcock appeared on the screen. I took the phone from her and looked carefully. He was 47, was born in Bristol but had gone to school in this area and from his pictures it seemed that his main interests were cars and beer.

'What do you think?' she asked again.

'Well, he seems to like cars,' I replied, cautiously.

'That's because he's a used car salesman, a dodgy used car salesman. He rips people off all the time,' she said.

'You want me to kill this guy because he's a dodgy car salesman? You don't have a car. You don't even drive!' I exclaimed.

'That's just a little insight into the kind of person he is,' she said. 'I don't want to talk about what else he's done.'

I stared at her. She looked serious, really serious. Those eyes of hers had never looked so intense.

'Bea, this is nuts,' I protested. 'It takes a certain kind of person to kill someone and I'm not it and I don't think you are either.' I shook my head. I knew she was a one-off but, even for her, this was extreme.

'Think about it,' she insisted. 'Think about what Brett did to you. Are you really okay with him getting away with it? You tried dealing with it the so-called right way and where did that get you? Why shouldn't we take things into our own hands?'

'Because even if we wanted to and we knew how to, we probably wouldn't get away with it,' I said.

She looked at me and shrugged. 'I don't understand why we're expected to quietly put up with all the terrible things that men like Dale and Brett do to us. I don't think they would.'

I looked at her, confused and doubtful.

'Look,' she said, 'I'm going to go home and give you a chance to think about it. I know it's a big deal. Take your time and we'll talk about it tomorrow.'

Once she'd gone, I realised she'd left the film in the DVD player. I went to take it out but instead I found myself watching it all over again.

NIGHTMARE

I woke to find mum sitting on the edge of my bed, gently stroking my forehead.

'What is it?' I murmured.

'You screamed out in your sleep. You must have been having a nightmare again,' she said.

I groaned. 'But I haven't had one for ages.'

'I know, but you had one just now. Would you like me to stay here with you?'

'No, I'll be fine,' I said. 'I don't even remember it. You go back to bed.'

She sat with me for a while and then she kissed me and left.

I lay there staring into the darkness. I shivered as I tried to control my thoughts. I did remember what I'd dreamt. It wasn't about me. It was about Bea and that Dale Tarrant guy on

Facebook. I put my arms over my eyes and sighed. 'Don't think about it,' I tried to tell myself. 'You don't even know what he did.'

I grabbed my normal phone from under the bed and turned it on and off and then on and off again. I put it away and laid back down. Bea had asked me to think about what Brett did to me and I really didn't want to but maybe I owed her that before I dismissed whatever crazy plan she had, entirely.

It had all started with Jazz and the long-term obsession she'd had with an older boy called Ollie. If we weren't hanging out with Andy at school breaktimes, then we were drifting over to Ollie's classroom so Jazz could make eyes at him. He never seemed into Jazz in that way but he was always happy to let us hang out with him and his mates, and that's how I first met Brett.

The first time I saw him, Jazz and I were sitting in an English lesson on the top floor of the main building. I was checking through my essay on war poetry before I handed it in and Jazz was busy day-dreaming out of the window, when suddenly she nudged me.

'Look, there's Ollie,' she said. 'Over by the pond.'

I looked over idly and then I looked again. 'Who's that with him?' I asked.

'Oh, that must be the new boy, Brett,' she said, casually. 'He's cute, isn't he?'

'And some,' I said. 'Look at him. He's like some kind of Tom Holland – KJ Apa lovechild.'

Jazz looked at me, surprised. 'I thought you were Little Miss It's All About Personality, Not Looks,' she laughed.

'I think I may have just discovered the exception,' I replied.

After that, I was as ridiculous as Jazz. Whenever we could, we went looking for Ollie and Brett. The only difference was, whereas before I'd been really relaxed around Ollie and his mates, now I was all tongue-tied and stupid. I don't think Brett even noticed me. I certainly wasn't the only girl that was interested in him. Maya and Tilly were always there now, giggling and flirting in that brash way that they had. I wasn't daft. I knew I wasn't going to get a look in. That seemed to change, though, one rainy lunchtime about a month later. It was one of those times when everyone's bored and restless and people start asking each other embarrassing questions for something to do. 'What's everyone's body count?' asked one of the boys.

The question went around the room and everyone said a number and then it got to me. I stood there awkwardly, wishing the ground would swallow me up. How could I admit that I didn't even know what they were talking about? What was a body count? I looked to Jazz for help and she whispered, 'How many people have you slept with?'

Shit, what was I supposed to say to that? I looked around the room and saw that everyone was staring at me, especially Brett. God, what would he want me to say? I figured the truth wouldn't impress him. If I told the truth, he'd just think I was a stupid, little kid and that was the last thing I wanted, so I lied. 'Two,' I piped up in a wobbly voice.

'Yeah, right,' said Maya. 'That's bullshit.' She laughed and so did the others except for Jazz and Brett. I looked at Brett and saw that he was looking at me curiously, one eyebrow raised. I shuddered under his gaze and was glad when the attention switched to Ollie, as he tried to pretend that he had a body count of a dozen.

'I don't know what you see in Ollie,' I said to Jazz, as we walked back to class. 'He's such a sleazy fuckboy sometimes.'

'That's just talk,' she said. 'He's not like that really. I don't think his body count is any more than yours.' She grabbed my arm and asked, 'Why did you lie?'

'I don't know. Because everyone lies in those situations. Because I didn't want to be humiliated. Because I didn't want anyone to think I was too innocent.'

'You mean you didn't want Brett to think you were too innocent,' clarified Jazz.

The following week was half-term. Andy was away with

Yannick and I spent most of the holiday round at Jazz's. It was on the Friday morning that we got the invitation to Ollie's party. Jazz was immediately downcast.

'I can't believe I finally get invited to Ollie's house and my parents aren't going to let me go,' she wailed.

'You don't know that,' I said. 'You haven't asked them yet.'

'I do know that,' she insisted. 'They're really into the whole virus thing. They won't let me do anything that breaks the rules.'

'But no-one is going to be at that party that we don't normally spend time with,' I reasoned.

'But we're not supposed to be spending time with them, are we? None of them are in our bubble. Plus, there's more than six of us in the group.'

'You're right,' I conceded, 'they're probably not going to let you go but you should still ask them.'

She left me in her room and went off to find them. She was gone a long time and I was starting to think that maybe she was managing to talk them round. One look at her face when she returned, though, soon set me right on that.

'Not good?' I asked.

'No, not good and a half-hour lecture on the irresponsibility of everybody else. Next time you have a stupid idea about me talking to my parents, keep it to yourself.'

'Sorry,' I said. 'I know they're strict and everything but they're pretty cool sometimes too.'

'They haven't been cool since I was thirteen,' Jazz pointed out. 'Some parents shouldn't be allowed teenagers. They don't understand them.'

I shrugged at her, apologetically. 'Do you mind if I go?' I asked, tentatively. 'I can stay here and keep you company if you'd rather.'

'No, you have to go,' she insisted. 'You shouldn't miss out just because I've got over-the-top parents. I'll just have to content myself with helping you look a million dollars.'

Later that night, I got an insta message from Brett which, at the time, seemed like the single most exciting thing that had ever happened to me. I didn't read it straight away. I didn't want to seem too keen. Then I did read it and then I made myself go and get a bite to eat before I replied.

'I'm good,' I messaged back, 'u?'

'Lookin forward to the party. u goin?' he replied.

'Yeah, Jazz can't make it but I'll be there,' I wrote.

'Shame, glad ur goin tho.'

'Thx.'

'U never seem very confident,' he messaged, 'but u should be. ur really hot'

'Thx, u2.'

'There can't be many boys who wouldn't want to jump your bones. I know I want to.'

I wasn't sure what to say to that, so I just sent a few kisses and called Jazz for an urgent chat.

The next morning, I woke up to half-a-dozen messages from him. All, but one, were dick pics. The last one said, 'your turn.' If it had been anyone else, I'd have aired him but it was Brett, so I said, 'thx, see you later.'

That evening, I went to Jazz's and we spent an hour or two getting ready, or pretending to get ready in Jazz's case. I didn't like to rush off and leave her too soon, so it was quite late by the time I got to Ollie's and the party was already lively. I thought he'd only invited a dozen people but word must have got out because there was at least twice that number there and it took me a while to make my way through them all and find Brett. I finally found him in a corner in the living room. He was sitting in an armchair, with Maya and Tilly perched either side of him. Shyly, I waved at him and he half-raised his eyebrows at me. I stood in the doorway hoping he'd break away from them and come and talk to me, but he didn't.

Ollie brushed past me on his way to the kitchen. 'Where's your drink?' he said. 'Come and get one.' I followed him through and watched as he poured me a vodka. He asked where Jazz was and seemed genuinely disappointed when I told him that her parents hadn't let her come. Then he moved on and found some other people to talk to. I wandered around some more, hoping that at some point Brett would appear by my side. I'd been wandering aimlessly for a good half hour when suddenly the music went off and someone shouted out, 'Everybody hide, it's the police.'

Most people fled upstairs but I dived into a back room with a couple of other people and, finally, there he was. We watched as the other people in the room squeezed themselves into a large wardrobe but there wasn't room for us as well. 'Never mind,' said Brett, as he closed the wardrobe door on them. 'I've got a better idea.' He pulled back a curtain and opened the window. Then he lifted me up onto the window ledge and told me to jump. It wasn't much of a drop but I jumped in such a hurry that I landed on my hands and knees. By the time I'd righted myself, Brett was standing beside me and pushing the window to. 'Do you see what I see?' he asked, eagerly.

I looked across the garden. Right at the back was a large tree with a ladder leaning against the trunk. I followed the ladder upwards with my eyes. It disappeared into a gloomy, square structure.

'A tree house,' I said.

'Exactly,' he said. 'A perfect hiding place.'

He grabbed my hand and led me to the ladder. He let me go up first and followed up behind. We stood together in the gloom, letting our eyes adjust. It was basically just a dusty, eight-foot cube with a little window in the far side.

'It's so dark,' I said.

'Not so dark I can't tell you're looking as peng as ever.' He leaned down and kissed me.

Briefly, my heart started to sing but then I felt his hands pressing down hard on my shoulders and his foot came around the back of my legs and took my feet from under me. I fell to the hard floor with a crash and my head banged on the log wall behind me. 'Stop it,' I cried, and tried to push him away. 'Shut up,' he hissed, and let all of his weight fall on top of me. I froze as he started to fumble with his trousers and I realised what was happening. Paralysed with fear, all I could do was close my eyes tight and count. All the time my head was banging against the log wall, I counted as it banged. I told myself that numbers go on forever and that this couldn't last that long and if I just focused on the numbers then it would all be over. I can't remember how high I counted or even if I counted in the right order but the numbers stayed with me and, eventually, I felt his weight leaving me. He pulled up his trousers and put his head close to mine. He smiled an ugly smile and said, 'don't forget those pics you owe me.' Then he was gone and I lay there, hurting all over, desperately wanting to be home and not daring to move.

HEROES

I woke late the next morning. Reliving the attack had thrown me and it had taken a long time to get back to sleep. I raised my groggy head and reached under the bed for my phones. There was an excited message from Andy with a picture of the most adorable staffie puppy. It was all white except for a black patch over one eye and it had a bright red bandana tied around its neck. 'Dad got me a rescue pup to cheer me up. Want to come over and help name him?' said the message. I was about to accept when the burner phone buzzed. I picked it up – it was a message from Bea. 'Can you meet me at the bus station at 11?' I looked at Andy's puppy pic and I looked at Bea's message. I remembered what she'd said the previous evening, 'Think about what Brett did to you. Are you really okay with him getting away with it?' I pictured that ugly smile of his and I knew that I wasn't okay with it. I really wasn't okay. I messaged Andy – 'sorry, can't make it, maybe tomorrow.'

It was an unexpectedly nice day outside and so I walked down the hill and along the river to the bus station. Bea was waiting for me on the corner. She grinned as she saw me and ran to meet me, sparking with nervous energy. 'You look tired,' she said, sympathetically, as she rubbed her head and flattened an unruly strand of hair.

'I didn't sleep well,' I said. 'What's going on? What have you got planned?'

She pulled my arm and led me towards bus stand 3. 'I thought we'd take the bus that goes along the river and have a picnic out at Stonebridge.' She tapped her bag as she spoke.

We joined a small queue of masked people and waited our turn to get on the bus. There were a few older people, a couple with a buggy and an anxious-looking boy who looked like he was dressed for an interview. We followed him up the spiral stairs. He took the front seat and so we headed for the back.

Bea took her mask off as soon as we sat down. 'Phew,' she said, 'I hate these things.'

'So, what food did you bring?' I asked.

'Crisps, wraps, the usual,' she said, 'and this.' She took out a small bar of chocolate, snapped it in two and offered me half.

I waved it away as she said, 'I've got something to tell you and I think you're going to be mad at me to start with, and then I hope it's going to be okay.'

I felt the hairs rise on the back of my neck again, and my mind leapt to the scene in the film where Bruno hides in the bushes waiting to tell Guy that he's murdered his wife.

'Don't look so horrified,' she said. 'It's not that awful.'

'So, what is it? What have you done?' I demanded.

'I messaged Brett,' she said, quickly.

'You did what?' I exclaimed.

''We need to know where he is, so I messaged him and we got talking and I found out that he's away training somewhere this week, and then he's going to be back at the barracks for a month.'

'And who did you say you were?' I asked.

'I set up a fake insta account in the name of Bonnie Bell,' she said, 'but I've deleted it now that we've got the information we need.'

I looked out of the window and muttered, 'You're supposed to have your mask on.' I was furious. How dare she contact that creep and start having conversations with him? How messed up was she?

Obediently, Bea put her face mask back on. 'I'm really sorry,' she said, 'but there is a greater purpose to this.'

I ignored her and continued looking in the other direction. The bus wound its way through the country lanes and crossed the river. There was a canoe drifting towards us and a small boy, sitting at the front of it, waved at me. I smiled back, weakly, beneath my mask.

When we finally got off the bus, I walked along the river a bit and sat on the bank. Bea followed me. 'I'm sorry,' she said, 'but I did it for you, for both of us. Brett and Dale are despicable bastards and if we don't do anything about them, nobody will.'

'I know Brett's a bastard but he's a bastard because of the way that he took away my power and my choice and, right now, that's what you're doing too. I need to have control over my life.'

'But that's what I'm trying to give you,' said Bea.

'Except that you're not. You're taking over and making decisions for me and I don't like it. Sometimes, I wish I'd never met you,' I protested.

I didn't look at her as I said it, but I could imagine the hurt in her eyes. She sat quietly beside me for a while and then she put her burner phone on the ground in front of me. 'I'm going to go for a walk up on the hill. If you still want to be friends, then come and join me when you're ready. If you don't, you can chuck our phones in the river and go home. Here's the bus ticket. You can have it.' She dropped the ticket in my lap and walked away.

I listened as her footsteps crossed the lane behind me and as she pushed her way through the bushes and up onto the hill. I sighed and looked up and down the river. There were a couple of swans swimming way down where the river bent away from view and a group of mallards just across the river from me. I picked up Bea's phone and held it to my head. I knew the sensible thing was to throw it in the river along with mine and go home. It might not be too late to go round to Andy's and meet that puppy. I sat a while longer and then jumped when an almighty quacking started in the water in front of me. I looked down and saw two drakes, fighting ferociously. They were flapping and splashing and pecking each other for all they were worth. I put down Bea's phone, picked up a stick and hurled it at them. They took no notice. Then I retrieved Bea's phone, crossed the road and started up the hill after her.

There was a bench perched like a tiara on the brow of the hill, but Bea wasn't on it. It wasn't until I'd almost reached it, that I saw her. She was a fair way down the other side, pacing and stamping, backwards and forwards, in the long grass. 'What are you doing?' I called down.

She looked up at the sound of my voice and her face broke into a huge smile. 'I'm writing a message for them down there,' she said, nodding her head down the hill and in the direction of Collington Barracks. I knew the barracks was there, it wasn't my first time visiting that place, but I still got the shivers, looking down on it.

'Kinda ruins the view, doesn't it?' said Bea.

'It really does,' I answered. 'Do they have to make them that ugly.'

'It's probably ugly by default rather than design,' she said.

'Probably,' I said.

'So, are we okay?' she asked, cautiously.

'Yes,' I said, 'if you tell me what you're writing.'

She ran up to the first marks that she'd made in the grass and called me over. 'Read it,' she said.

I spelled it out, 'R-A-P-I-S-T-S,' I said, as I walked along underneath the letters.

'Now come down a line,' she said.

I moved a few feet down towards the barracks and started reading again, 'C-A-N-T B-E.'

'And I'm just doing the last bit now,' she called, as she ran a little further down the hill.

I joined her on the last level of her message. 'H-E-R- heroes,' I said. 'Rapists can't be heroes.'

'Exactly. Rapists can't be heroes. This would work a lot better if this hill was made of chalk and the message could be seen from the barracks but I just wanted to write it, even if it can't be seen. I hope you don't mind,' she said, tentatively.

'I don't mind,' I said. 'In fact, I'll help you.'

While she finished the letters for 'heroes,' I jumped up and down on the other letters, trying to impress them more deeply into the ground.

Once we'd finished, we sat on the bench.

'I'm really glad you didn't leave me,' said Bea, 'because I think we make a pretty good team. We sorted Brady out all right, didn't we?'

'We did,' I agreed.

'And it was fun?'

'And it was fun,' I conceded.

'So, does this mean we can go ahead with Operation Justice?'

'It depends what you mean by Operation Justice. I want Brett to suffer some consequence for what he did, but all this talk about killing is nuts. There's got to be a middle way.'

'Like half-killing him,' she suggested.

'Something like that,' I smiled.

I looked down at the base again. There were a lot of squat, square, uninspiring buildings surrounded by tall fences and barbed wire and security cameras. A sentry stood by a huge metal gate.

'So, do you think that guy has got a gun?' I asked.

'I expect so,' replied Bea.

A group of soldiers appeared and assembled in the middle of the base where they began doing drills.

'What are they supposed to be protecting us from, anyway?' I said.

'Terrorism, cyberterrorism, China, Russia, stuff like that, I guess.'

'So, who's supposed to be protecting us from the people that are actually dangerous to us?' I asked.

'That's what I've been trying to tell you. That's down to us. The army won't do it, the police don't do much and the government doesn't care. Men like Dale and Brett and Brady aren't a threat to the people who get to make the decisions,' explained Bea.

'Do you think they'd do more about it if they were?'

'I'm sure they would,' she replied.

The sentry marched to the other side of the gate and back again.

'What sort of gun do you think he's got?' I asked.

'I don't know, but I don't think it's a water pistol.'

'In that case, unless you're planning on raining burning arrows down there or you've got a Trojan Horse up your sleeve, I don't see how you're going to get anywhere near Brett,' I said.

She waved her phone at me. 'That's where you're wrong. We can get anywhere we want to with this.'

'You have a plan already, don't you?'

She nodded, mysteriously.

'Bea, just tell me what it is,' I said, impatiently.

'Well, I thought that, if you're happy with it,' she glanced up at me, 'we could test my theory that the most predatory men are also the most homophobic men and we could use that against them. I think that some men are homophobic because they're afraid of being on the receiving end of the kind of behaviour that they dish out.'

'Is that true?' I asked.

'I don't know but it makes some sense, doesn't it?' she said.

'So, what do we do?'

'We use these,' she waved her phone again, 'to send Brett and

Dale provocative messages from each other.' She paused and smiled mischievously at me.

'And then what happens?' I asked.

'They get more and more wound up until they want to beat each other's brains out and then we organise that for them.'

'So, we don't actually have to do much at all? Just send a few messages?' I said.

'Exactly, we use their weaknesses against them and we make sure we're several steps removed from whatever happens. To the rest of the world, it will just be a fight between two stupid men. What do you think?'

'I think I like it, but how exactly would it work?' I asked.

'We set up a fake account on my phone with a name like Randy or Chase or something and we message Brett with pictures and suggestive comments and hopefully he gets riled up and aggressive and then we do a similar thing to Dale on your phone. We pretend Brett's looking for a sugar daddy.'

'But won't they see through it or think it's their mates winding them up? Why would they believe it?' I questioned.

'Why do people believe anything? Why do they believe they might win the lottery or that there's a God? People believe what they want to believe and sometimes they want to believe the thing that makes them angry.'

I nodded and then I thought a bit more and looked at her, quizzically. 'So, you believe in lake monsters but not in God then?'

'Lake monsters just seem a whole lot more plausible and, anyway, I know for sure there isn't any kind of God looking out for me. The whole God thing just doesn't add up.'

'What do you mean?'

'Isn't God supposed to have limitless power and boundless compassion and infinite knowledge? That doesn't make any sense. Think about it. If you were creating people, would you make one sex physically stronger than the other, less empathetic than the other and more sexually-driven than the other? You don't have to have infinite knowledge to know that that's not going to end well for everybody.'

DALE

The next day, I did go to Andy's and I met the puppy, who'd been named Patch in my absence. Jazz was there too and we took Patch for a walk in the park and lapped up all the attention he got from passers-by. Turned out puppies and social distancing are not a natural combination. My mind was buzzing from Bea's grand plan but Jazz and Andy were used to me being preoccupied and didn't seem to mind my erratic presence. When they weren't talking about Andy's pending court date, they were busy chatting school stuff, anyway – the school play, the new uniform rules and all those things that seemed really distant to me now. I was about to head back home when Jazz pulled me to one side. 'Can I talk to you a minute?' she asked.

'Of course, what is it?'

'I've got something I have to tell you and I know I should have told you already but I didn't know how to say it because I'm not sure how you'll feel about it,' she said, confusingly.

'Then just say it and stop scaring me,' I told her.

'It's about me and Ollie.'

'You and Ollie?'

'Yeah, we're kind of a thing, a kind of definite kind of a thing,' she said.

'A thing?' The words echoed in my head. 'Since when?'

'About seven months,' she replied, nervously.

I did the maths. 'So that means ...?'

'Yes,' she said awkwardly. 'He came round my house the day after the party and said that he'd really missed me and things kind of went from there.'

'That's great,' I said, flatly. 'I'm happy for you.'

'Thanks,' she said, looking relieved. 'That means a lot.'

Thoughts and memories exploded in my head as I walked home. Seven months ago. Wow! I knew it was supposed to be childish to say that life's not fair, but it really fucking wasn't! Life shouldn't make one friend's dreams come true at exactly the same time that it stamps all over the other friend. Should it?

I was still in a funk when Bea came round that evening. I made us noodles and, once we'd eaten, Bea put her burner phone in the middle of the table. Resolutely, I placed mine next to it.

'Are you sure you want to do this?' asked Bea, warily.

'Don't worry about me,' I assured her. 'I am so up for this now.'

'Good,' she said. 'That's really good to hear. Let's get started. We're going to have to do this on Facebook because Dale is too old to be on insta or snap. Luckily, Brett has a Facebook account too.'

'Does he use it?' I asked.

'He seems to. He's posted a few action army shots in the last month. Now, we just have to set up fake accounts. You set one up for Randy and I'll be Chase.' She slid my phone back across the table to me.

It took longer than I thought it would, partly because we didn't have any pictures of Chase or Randy and partly because neither of us had any idea what other kinds of pictures a Chase or a Randy might want to post. We tried an app that turned our own faces into male faces but mine wasn't very convincing and Bea took one look at hers, deleted it and refused to talk about it any further. In the end, we went for a series of super sporty cars for Chase's profile pictures and guns and a tank for Randy's.

'Time to start messaging,' said Bea, once the pages were all set up.

'Aren't we going to have to do some research if we want to be convincing?' I said. 'We don't know anything about being gay or about being a pest.'

'As far as we know, they don't know anything about the gay scene either so we've got a bit of leeway there,' said Bea. 'It's being convincing creeps that we really need to get right.'

'Should we start with dick pics then?' I suggested. 'Have you got any on your phone that we could use?'

'All deleted,' she said. 'What about you?'

'Brett sent me some,' I said, hesitantly. 'I'll have to unblock him to access them but I could do that temporarily. They're on my other phone. I'll just get it.'

I got the phone and searched for the few messages that Brett had sent me. 'Are you sure you're okay with this?' asked Bea.

'Yes, I'm okay. Definitely. Which burner phone should I send them to?'

'Both, we'll send one pic to each of them for now,' said Bea.

I was puzzled. 'But won't Brett recognise it's his own dick he's been sent a picture of?'

'I don't know. I don't know what angle he normally looks at it from or if he lovingly gazes at a picture like that every bedtime and kisses it goodnight. And even if he does, that'll just play around with his head more. He'll have to compare it with his own pics and, even then, he won't know if he's got a dick double or not.'

'I guess if he does think it's his, Chase can say that he's got loads more and he's going to post them to Brett's parents or something,' I suggested.

'Or his commanding officer and all his regiment,' said Bea. 'Okay, mine have come through and I'm going to send this one. Are you ready to DM?'

'I'm ready,' I smiled. 'Let's do this.'

So, we did. We sent Brett a pic from Chase, with the message, 'Wanna piece of this, soldier boy?' Then we sent Dale a pic from Randy and wrote underneath, 'When do I get to drive your car, sugarbear?'

'Now we wait,' said Bea, 'and it might take a while. In the meantime, I think we should have a drink to commemorate this moment. Have you got anything suitable?'

I opened the fridge and had a look. 'All we've got is some orange juice and a little bit of sparkling water left in this bottle. Will that do?'

Bea said she thought that it would, so I made up the drinks and handed her a glass.

'To Operation Justice,' she said, gravely.

'To Operation Justice,' I repeated.

I checked my burner phone, first thing the next morning, but there was no reply on Randy's Facebook page. I called Bea and she'd not heard anything either. It was the same the next day and it was all starting to feel like a bit of an anti-climax. Maybe, neither of them would take the bait.

It was on the third day that Bea called me, her voice full of excitement. 'We're in business. Brett has seen his message and he's not a happy boy.'

'What did he say?' I asked.

'Just a sec, let me read it to you. He said, 'Fuck the fuck right off or you won't recognise your fuckin dick when I've finished with it.'"

'Wow, I didn't think it would work that well. He's seriously pissed off. What should we say back?'

'Chase is thinking of saying, 'That's what I was hoping. Here's another pic to whet your appetite. You owe me one. I'm waiting.'"

'Chase seems to really know what he's doing. Go for it,' I told her.

Bea came over again at the weekend. There had been another couple of responses from Brett by then, but still nothing from Dale. Bea was getting worried. 'This will only work if they're both responding, and if Dale takes too long, then Brett might have gotten over himself and let it go.'

I checked the Randy Facebook page. 'Dale still hasn't looked at it,' I said. 'If we were Facebook, we could send him a notification to give him a nudge, but we're not.'

Bea thought for a minute and then her face lit up. 'We could give him an old-school poster board nudge, though.'

'What would that involve?' I asked.

'Well, I know where his garage is. It's on the other side of town. We, or you, because if I did it, he might recognise me, could go and walk up and down outside his garage with a Facebook poster board on your back.'

'Do you honestly think that would work. I can't see it,' I said, sceptically.

'But it might do. It is how advertising works, after all. It's got to be worth a shot now that we've got this far. Randy will be disappointed if we don't,' said Bea.

'You mean, if I don't,' I corrected her.

'I'd do it if I could. I'd do it if it was the other way around,' she assured me.

'You'd go marching around Collington Barracks wearing a Facebook advert? They'd think you were on some kind of weird protest and you'd get arrested or something,' I said.

'I would do it, and I will do it, if that's what it takes. Watch me!'

'Okay,' I sighed. 'I'll do it, but where do we get the Facebook advertising from?'

'I guess we'll have to make it. We just need some big bits of cardboard and blue and white paint. Any chance you've got that? You've got blue walls in the hallway so you might have some paint left over,' suggested Bea.

We checked the garage and we were in luck. We found some flattened cardboard boxes in one corner of the garage and some old paint tins nearby and, sure enough, there was blue and there was white. We cut our boards, and then Bea sketched out the Facebook 'f' on one of them and 'Facebook' on the other. While she did that, I got a couple of paintbrushes from the drawer in the kitchen. Then she opened the paint tins, took the smallest paintbrush and began painting in the letters. I used the bigger brush and covered everything else in blue. The slowest part of the procedure was waiting for the paint to dry. It was four o'clock by the time Bea was finally satisfied that it was ready. Then she turned to me, pleadingly, 'You know if we hurried, we could probably get across town and nudge him today?'

An hour and two buses later, I was standing foolishly in a little recreation ground while Bea attached the tops of the boards with string and then hung them over my neck.

'How do I look?' I asked, uncomfortably.

'Divine,' she said. 'Mark Zuckerberg would be proud of you. I'll get him to send you a commission.'

She pointed me in the direction of Dale's garage. It involved a couple of turns and crossing the road but it wasn't too far. The road was busy and it took a while to get across. I got tooted at as I dashed between a couple of cars when the traffic slowed, but I was relieved to find most people ignored me. As I approached the garage, I could see Dale talking animatedly to a customer on the forecourt. This was the difficult bit. I needed him to see the boards but I didn't want him to notice me particularly. I walked down the road a bit and then back again. I saw him glance at me and all I could do was hope the boards were more interesting to him than I was. I crossed the road and went back and forth on the other side. I'd just crossed back again when I heard a couple of voices calling me.

I looked around and saw Andy, Patch and Jazz heading in my direction.

'I was sure it was you,' called Andy. 'Jazz wouldn't believe me.' He looked me up and down as they got closer. 'That's a pretty weird outfit you're rocking. What are you doing?'

I said hello to Patch who kept trying to jump at me and scraped bits of paint off the sign as he fell back down. What was I doing? That was a good question. Would they believe me if I told them Facebook was paying me to do some advertising for them? I looked down at the less than pristine 'f' and knew that that was completely unbelievable.

115

'I'm doing this confidence-building programme,' I lied. 'It's for kids who've been struggling with school. You get different challenges every day and you get points if you manage to do them. It starts off with things like going to the shops and catching buses and then it works up to more attention-grabbing challenges like this one.'

Jazz looked impressed. 'Does that mean you'll be ready to come back to school soon?'

'Well, I've got a few more challenges to work through before I'll be ready for that.'

'Like what?' she asked.

'I don't know, singing in the park, that sort of thing.'

'Walking through the high street in your mum's dressing gown,' suggested Andy.

'Oi,' a voice snarled suddenly, from behind us. 'What do you think you're doing?'

We spun around and there was Dale bearing down on us. 'We're talking,' said Andy.

'Well, while you've been having your little mothers' meeting, your dog has been shitting on my forecourt. Now, clear it up.'

Andy took out a poo bag and picked up Patch's poo while Dale stood over him, menacingly. He was breathing heavily and a vein palpitated visibly on the left side of his scarred and blotchy face.

'Now, fuck off and take your shitty dog with you,' said Dale, as Andy straightened up.

'I don't think that guy likes me much,' said Andy, as soon as we were out of earshot.

'Don't take any notice, Andy. He's a colossal jerk,' said Jazz.

I didn't say anything. I was shocked. I'd been expecting him to be a creep but he was scarily aggressive and I still didn't know what he'd done to Bea.

At the end of the road, I told them I'd got to go and meet my mum somewhere and then I doubled back to the little park where Bea was waiting for me. I told her what had happened and she grimaced. I noticed her knuckles whitening as she grabbed hold of the boards and took them off me. 'I told you he was a lowlife, didn't I?' was all she said.

Walking up and down the road in a sandwich board still seems like a stupid thing to have done, but it worked. Not immediately, but within a few hours. I checked the burner phone later that night and there it was. A message from Dale. Having seen how easily riled he was, I shouldn't have been too surprised. 'I'm gonna rip your dick off and shove it where the sun don't shine, arsehole!!' it said. Wow, this was going to be easy. I called Bea who was delighted with the success of her plan. We talked about how to reply and decided just to send another dick pic with a question mark. He really was a very easy man to wind up.

Things carried on like that for the next few days. Chase and Randy had fun sending lewd pics and messages to Brett and Dale, and Brett and Dale reliably exploded. It was like they were marionette puppets and all we had to do was pull the right strings to get them convulsing.

STRANGE BEHAVIOUR

I made more of an effort to see Jazz and Andy after our unexpected meeting at Dale's garage. I felt terrible for having lied to them so readily. I tried to play that whole challenge story down as quickly as I could. I told them I'd done as much as I could for now and I was going to leave it for a bit. Jazz was disappointed as she was hoping I was working towards going back to school. I wasn't. I did start meeting them after school most days, though, so we could all walk Patch together. We were walking him in Victoria Park one day when we rounded a corner and nearly collided with Bea. I opened my mouth to say 'hi' but she blanked me, just walked on by. I looked back, shocked.

'Do you know that girl?' asked Jazz.

'I'm not sure,' I said, 'she reminds me of someone.'

'Someone who's full of themselves by any chance?' asked Jazz. 'She was the one who almost walked into us and she didn't say sorry or anything.'

'I know,' I said, puzzled. Surely, Bea had seen me, hadn't she?

Was this all part of the burner phone, no names, no-one who knows us can ever see us together subterfuge that she was so into?

Andy and Jazz were in the school play, and rehearsal times had had to be brought forward to accommodate Andy's curfew times, so it wasn't long before they had to leave. That worked perfectly for me. I said goodbye to them at the park gates and went straight back into the park. I could see Bea, in her sky-blue shirt and her pink cap, sitting on a bench on the far side. I headed slowly in her direction but I wasn't sure if I should approach her or not. I didn't think she'd snub me again, not now that I was on my own, but I wasn't entirely sure.

I was still umming and ahing when a man walked quickly past me, circled Bea's bench and then sat down, about three feet away from her. I watched them as they glanced at each other and then seemed to look very deliberately in opposite directions. She moved first. She got an envelope out of her pocket and pushed it towards him. Quickly, he swooped it up and put a package in its place. Bea picked up her rucksack with one hand and moved her other hand towards the package. Deftly, she pushed the package into the opening of the bag and put the bag back on the ground. They both sat there a moment longer and then he got up and started walking back in my direction.

I stared at him as he went past. Who was he and what had he just given to Bea? Most of the 'roadmen' I knew were just pretending to be tough but this guy looked like he was the real deal. He had the textbook look – fancy black clothes and a big silver chain, and he reeked of weed. It was the impenetrably cold expression on his face that gave me the chills, though. I stood to one side to let him go by and then I noticed that Bea was getting up. I stepped behind the nearest tree and watched as she left the park from the south side. It would have all made sense if Bea was into drugs, but she wasn't. She thought they were lame.

I didn't message her until I got home. She had me on Snap Maps and I didn't want her to suspect I'd been spying on her. 'Hey, how are you?' she messaged back.

'I'm good. Mum's working. You up for a movie night?' I asked.

'Sure. Give me two hours. I'll bring a film,' she replied.

Good as her word, she arrived two hours later.

'What a day,' she said, as I let her in. 'I'm looking forward to losing myself in a good movie and bad food. What about you?'

'My day was fine,' I said. 'I was in the park earlier.'

I expected her to say that she was there too and give me some kind of explanation but instead she said, 'Oh, what was it like there today? Was it busy?'

She put her rucksack on the table, took a DVD out of the front compartment and went to put it on.

'Shall I get some snacks?' I asked.

'I've got popcorn in my bag,' she replied.

I moved towards her bag and was about to pick it up when she ran and jumped in front of me saying, 'I'll get it. You get us a bowl and some drinks.' I hesitated and she hesitated and then I did what she'd said. When I returned from the kitchen, the popcorn was sitting on the table and her rucksack was nowhere to be seen.

She tipped the popcorn into the bowl, grabbed her drink and flopped onto the sofa. 'You ready?' she said.

I joined her and pressed play. The movie was called *Brave Bessie* and it was a true story. It was about a woman called Bessie Coleman who spent her childhood picking cotton with her family in Texas. Once she'd grown up, she moved to Chicago which was where she first heard stories about French women who could fly planes. She was fascinated and resolved to learn herself, but in America no-one would teach you if you were African-American, Native-American or a woman so that was her out three times over. She worked extra jobs, saved up, learned French, found someone to sponsor her, went to Paris and, in 1921, she became the first black woman to get her pilot's license. She went back to America and travelled the country as a stunt flier. She thrilled the crowds as she looped the loop, flew figure eights, walked on the wings, hung off bits of the plane and broke her ribs occasionally. Then on a practice flight in Florida, one day, she went up really high and, all of a sudden, her plane nosedived and span out of control. I gasped in horror as I watched her fall out of the spiralling, plummeting plane. I looked round at Bea to share the terrifying moment with her and she was fast asleep. I guess she really did have quite a day.

Once the film was over and I'd covered Bea up with a blanket, I thought about looking for her rucksack. Then I imagined her waking up and discovering me rifling through its contents and it didn't seem worth it. Bea had her reasons for being mysterious and, curious as I was, I didn't really want to pry into her deepest, darkest secrets any more than I wanted her to pry into mine.

THE PLAN

Bea seemed more like her normal self the next morning. Over tea and toast, we checked out Operation Justice. Dale and Brett had both sent outraged messages overnight. I read Dale's out, 'By the time I've finished redesigning your face, pretty boy, you're going to wish it was the fucking Taliban had got their hands on you.'

I read it again to myself and commented, 'I think he's getting more subtle.'

'You're right, he is,' said Bea. 'He seems to be putting more thought into it, which is more than I can say for Brett. Are you ready for his latest?'

'Tell me,' I said.

'Fuck right off. After I've put a bullet in your head, I'm going to set fire to all your cars and drive them off a cliff,' she read.

'I don't think he thought that one through,' I grimaced.

'Maybe he'd just got back from a forty-eight-hour night hike and his brain was all in shreds,' Bea suggested. 'Good to know the defence of the realm is in such capable hands, though.'

I laughed. 'So, what do we do next? I'm bored of sending dick pics now. I can't believe they're still reacting to them.'

'You're right, if we don't do something else, they're going to lose interest eventually. We need to bring things to a head while they're still so keen to tear each other apart,' she said.

'What have you got in mind?'

'I'm thinking the bench at the top of the hill overlooking the barracks, on Monday night. We just need to get them there and let them do the rest,' Bea said. 'Are you okay with that?'

'What do you think they'll do to each other?' I asked.

'By the looks of these messages, there isn't a lot that they don't want to do to each other.'

We sat for a while, scratching our heads and trying to compose the most perfectly provocative messages that we could. It wasn't as easy as we thought. Getting them to sound off at each other was one thing. Getting them so mad that they'd actually make the effort to go and meet each other wasn't quite so guaranteed. We made a long list of possibilities and finally managed to agree on two.

'Right,' said Bea, picking up her phone. 'So, Brett's last message to Chase said, 'Fuck right off. After I've put a bullet in your head, I'm going to set fire to all your cars and drive them off a cliff."

She looked up at me, 'What did we decide for Chase's reply?'

'Time to stop talking and prove yourself, soldier boy. If you're as hard as you like to think you are meet me at the top of Collington Hill, Monday night at 11. You're gonna find you're not the only one who's got a weapon that's ready and waiting.'

'Brilliant,' she said, once she'd finished typing. 'Let's do Randy's and then we can get them sent.'

I read Dale's message again. 'By the time I've finished redesigning your face, pretty boy, you're going to wish it was the fucking Taliban had got their hands on you.'

And then I typed in Randy's reply. 'You don't mean that, sugarbear. Meet me at the top of Collington Hill, Monday night at 11 and I'll show you why all the nice boys love a soldier.'

I looked at Bea and asked, 'Do you think that will work?'

'Only one way to find out. Are you ready? Three, two, one, send.'

We were just high-fiving in celebration when we heard a key turn in the lock.

'Shit,' cried Bea, as she jumped up. 'Your mum's home early. Where can I hide?'

'My bedroom,' I said, and she grabbed her shoes and ran for the back of the house.

Mum called 'hi' to me as she stopped in the hallway to take off her shoes and hang up her coat. Quickly, I scanned the room for any evidence of Bea. I put our breakfast plates and cups in the sink and was just grabbing the blanket from the sofa when mum walked in.

Mum looked at the blanket. 'Did you get cold last night?' she asked.

'Yeah, I was watching a movie till late and it got a bit chilly,' I said. 'How was your night?'

'Not great. That woman, Eileen, I told you about. She wouldn't settle again. Had me up and down all night.'

'You must be tired,' I said, sympathetically. 'Are you going straight to bed?'

'I'm going to jump in the shower first. Any chance you could make me a cup of tea while I'm in there?' she asked.

'Of course,' I replied. I went to the kitchen and made a cup of tea and found a couple of the really nice biscuits that were hidden at the back of the cupboard. I put them on a little plate and took it all through to mum's room. Then I went to check on Bea. I crossed the hallway, opened my bedroom door and felt the cold air blowing in from the open window. Bea was gone.

I went back to the kitchen and got myself a biscuit. Mum called me as she came out of the bathroom.

'What is it?' I asked.

'I've just remembered it's Lucy's birthday at the weekend and I haven't sent her a card yet. Could you get one from the stationery cupboard and write it and put it in the post for me? Please!'

'Okay,' I called back. 'I'll do it, don't worry.' The stationery cupboard was underneath the telly. I opened it and sitting on top of all the paper and cards and envelopes and things was Bea's rucksack. I pulled it out and took it to my room where I found a new hiding place for it, under the bed. Then I sat on the floor and stared at it. I felt like a kid who'd found their Xmas presents all wrapped up and was trying to work out the ethics of investigating them. Was it okay to feel the bag? To open it and glimpse in? To open it and put my hand in?

'I'm off to bed now,' shouted mum. 'Have you done that card yet?'

'Just doing it,' I called back.

I left my meditation on the bag and went and found a suitably floral card for Aunt Lucy. I scrawled a greeting in it and headed for the post office. It was busy and I had to join the queue outside. I was just putting my mask on, to enter the building, when my phone buzzed. I looked down. It was a message from Bea. 'Have you seen my rucksack?):'

'Don't worry,' I messaged back. 'I've put it somewhere safe. Has Brett replied yet?'

'Not yet. Dale?'

'No, I'll let you know when he does.'

Once I was done in the post office, I wasn't sure what to do. If I went home, I'd have to be quiet because mum was sleeping and then it would just be me and the bag. I messaged Jazz instead. 'Hey, you doing anything?'

She replied straight away, 'Andy's mum is taking us to the woods to walk Patch. Want to come?'

'Sure, where shall I meet you?'

'Andy's at 10.30.'

THE WOODS

It was a twenty-minute drive out to the woods. We went there a lot when we were kids and Jazz always used to have her birthday parties there. We'd play tracking games and chasing games and then there'd be a huge treasure hunt at the end. I hadn't been out there for a long time, though.

Once we got there, Andy's mum dropped us at the main car park and said she'd pick us up in three hours. We set off on the main track, towards the clearing where Jazz's parties used to be. The path was strewn with autumn leaves and the mushrooms that dotted either side of it were well past their best. Parts of brightly coloured fly agarics were littered here and there and the clumps of common inkcaps were turning to a slimy brown mush. Patch ran on ahead, sniffing and spraying everything in sight and chasing all the noises in the bushes.

'He's having the time of his life,' said Andy.

'It is a bit like dog paradise here,' I agreed.

'He was desperate to come out earlier but I had a Zoom appointment with my lawyer first thing this morning,' he continued.

'And are they going to lock you up and throw away the key?' asked Jazz.

'He says no-one will want to lock up schoolboys for such minor offences,' he explained. 'If I'm lucky, I'll get a conditional discharge or, if I'm really lucky, the charges will get thrown out of court. Otherwise, I'll get a fine, and I've got loads of people who've said they'll help me with that, or community payback, which I don't mind doing.'

'What if they're really mean and they make you clear land for a new road or runway or something, though?' said Jazz.

'Then, I'll refuse to do it,' said Andy, defiantly.

'What were the police like when they arrested you?' I asked. 'Didn't they mind having to arrest you when you'd hardly done anything wrong?'

'Some did, some didn't. There was an older policeman who was quite macho and old-school and he was keen to tell us what a menace to society we are. Then there was a policewoman who was a bit blinkered and really didn't understand why we did what we did. Yannick thinks she must be hot-braining with the Home Secretary. Some of the others seemed a bit embarrassed, though. They knew we had a good reason for hanging those banners up and that, as crimes go, it really wasn't much of one but they had to go along with orders. I feel sorry for them. I might be on night curfew, but at least I'm not on thought curfew.'

We rounded a bend in the path and saw the river ahead. 'Hey,' yelled Andy, 'do you remember this?' He ran ahead with an excited Patch at his heels. He ran at the river and jumped off the bank and out of sight. We waited for the splash but there was none and then we remembered Andy and the rope swing. You couldn't get him off it when he was little. We ran to join him and found that he'd shinned up the rope and was hanging onto the branch that the rope was attached to.

'I've not lost my skills,' he said, happily. 'Do you remember when we used to get three or four kids swinging at a time? We could probably still do that. Catch the rope and you two get on and then I'll slide down as you swing.' He swung the rope over to us. I sat on the stick and Jazz climbed on my shoulders. 'Ready, swing,' shouted Andy. I pushed my feet back and let go and we all went flying everywhere. I went forwards with the swing, Jazz fell off my shoulders and landed on the bank and Andy came tumbling down the rope at a rate of knots. He bounced off me and landed flat on his face in the water. Patch went berserk and barked wildly while I swung backwards and forwards like a pendulum until I lost momentum. I came to a halt, suspended over the middle of the river. 'I think we used to be a bit better at this,' said Andy, as he stood up, grabbed the rope and pulled me back to the side. We all climbed up the bank and Patch jumped excitedly at Andy as he squeezed out his clothes.

'I guess we're not as young as we used to be,' said Jazz.

'Uh-uh, you're not as young as you used to be. I am the same daredevil boy that I always was. Just find me that tree we always used to climb and I'll show you.'

'The one where you used to terrify my dad by going all the way to the top?' asked Jazz.

'That's the one,' replied Andy.

We walked on until we found Andy's tree and he immediately started climbing it while Patch ran around the bottom of it, barking frantically. 'Take a picture of me,' Andy shouted down to Jazz.

'Your dog's getting separation anxiety,' I called up the tree.

'Can't you distract him?' Andy shouted back.

Jazz and I sat under the tree and began throwing sticks for Patch which kept him quiet for a while.

'Your parties used to be so much fun, do you remember?' I asked her.

'Yeah, I loved them,' she replied.

'Do you remember that time your parents brought sledges and we went mud-sledging on that bare hill on the other side of the wood? And that other time when we were tracking and someone said that the prints we were following were from a wild boar?' I reminisced.

'Yeah, and then there was a huge animal on the path ahead of us and we all panicked because we thought it was a wild boar,' she continued.

'And most of us ran and climbed up the nearest tree but you completely froze.'

'And you were all calling me but I just couldn't make my body move,' she said.

'And then one of the bigger boys climbed down the tree and went and stood with you and held your hand,' I recalled.

'And then when the animal turned around and ran at us both, he stood in front of me and he was the one who got knocked over and I was okay,' she said.

'And then the wild boar turned out to be an over-friendly mastiff,' I laughed. 'Who was the boy who went and stood with you, do you remember?'

'It was Ollie,' she said.

'Really?' I said, surprised. 'So, is that the big attraction? He's your Prince Charming.'

'It's more than that,' she said. 'I know you think he's an idiot sometimes but I know that deep-down he's courageous and kind. When he's not trying to be cool and impress the other boys, that's the kind of person he really is.'

I looked at her. 'You really love him?' I asked.

'Yes,' she said. 'I do.'

'I'm happy for you,' I told her, meaning it this time. 'Truly.'

'You'll meet someone amazing as well, one day. I know you will.'

'I don't know about that,' I said. 'He'll have to be a lot more than amazing, but I'm not thinking about boys right now. For now, I could be happy with shares in Patch, if Andy's willing.'

ENDGAME

'Where have you been?' demanded Bea, when I finally got home and called her. 'I've been calling you half the day.'

'Sorry, I went to the woods and I turned off my phone,' I explained. 'What's going on?'

'Chase has got a reply from Brett,' she said, 'and it's perfect. Listen to this – 'You're on, but don't bother booking a return ticket because you won't be fucking needing it.''

'That's great,' I said, 'Let me check Randy's.' I went on to Randy's Facebook and clicked on messages.

'Well,' asked Bea, impatiently. 'Is there anything?'

'Yes, Dale says, 'Take one last look at your pretty face cause even mummy isn't going to recognise it.' That means he's going to go, doesn't it?'

'Yes,' said Bea, jubilantly, 'it does, we've done it or at least we've nearly done it. I can't believe it.'

'So, what now?' I asked.

'There's a late bus that goes that way on a Monday. It leaves at 9.30. I'm going to catch that,' she said.

'Do we have to be there?' I said. 'Surely, our work is done.'

'You don't, but I want to see what happens. If I don't go, we'll probably never get to hear about it.'

'But how are you going to get back again?' I asked.

'I'll walk,' she said.

'But it's miles and it'll be dark,' I protested.

'And ...?' she said.

'And I'm coming with you. I can't let you do that on your own. Mum's home on Monday but I'll tell her that I'm staying at Andy's or something.'

'You shouldn't come. I'll be fine on my own. You know I will. I don't want to have to worry about you getting caught up in things and getting hurt,' she argued.

'And I don't want you to start making decisions for me again,' I said. 'I'm coming whether you like it or not.'

'Okay, but you've got to promise me you're going to stay well away from the top of the hill,' she insisted.

'I promise,' I agreed.

After that, I didn't see Bea again until the big day. At 8.30 on the Monday evening, she called me to say she was just down the road, waiting for me, and to be sure not to forget her rucksack. I got it out from under the bed. I hadn't even thought about looking at it, since we'd finalised our plans, and I didn't have time now. Bea was sounding extremely tense and impatient.

We got to the bus station twenty minutes early, and Bea paced up and down while we waited for the bus to come in. Luckily, it was on time because I don't know what she would have done otherwise. I followed her onto the bus and, once we'd paid, we made our way to the seats at the back. As we pulled out of the station, I could feel Bea sitting rigidly beside me as she clasped her bag in front of her and peered fiercely out of the window. She took her mask off and breathed mist onto the window. Then she drew two conkers with their strings intertwined. I got out my burner phone and started looking through all the messages between Randy and Dale.

'Can I see yours?' I asked.

'My what?'

'Your phone?' I said.

'Why?'

'So, I can remind myself how we got to this point.'

She passed me her phone.

I typed in her password and found the Chase and Brett messages. When I got to the bottom, something seemed not quite right. I checked my phone again. It wasn't right.

'Bea,' I said. 'We've given them different times. I thought we agreed 11pm, but you've put 10.45 on Chase's message to Brett.'

She looked. 'Oh, well,' she said. 'I must have made a mistake. It's close enough. Don't worry about it.'

Once we got to our stop and jumped off the bus, Bea set about looking for a hiding place for me. I started to say I was happy to come up the hill with her but she reminded me, sharply, of my promise not to.

'Dale is likely to park his car here when he comes,' she said, 'so we've got to find you a good hiding place and you've got to stay in it. We don't want his car lights picking you out as he pulls up. Damn, none of these bushes are thick enough.'

I crossed the road and looked down at the river. There were three or four steps by the bridge that led down to the water and there was a little ledge underneath the bridge. 'Bea,' I called. 'What about here?'

'Perfect,' she said, once she'd checked it out. 'You go down there now and I'll make sure you can't be seen.'

Down I went and tried to make myself comfortable. I shimmied along underneath the bridge and then sat down. There was just enough room for me to be able to sit cross-legged on the cold, damp ledge. 'Now don't move until I get back,' said Bea. 'See you later.'

She left and I sat there in the dark, listening to the river flow by. I heard the hoot of an owl and saw what might have been a bat flying over the river. A car rumbled over the bridge and I jumped, but it turned and kept going once it got to the other side. It can't have been him. I leaned my head back against the bridge and felt something cold and slimy brush against my hand. I looked down apprehensively. Whatever it was jumped into the water and I thought I saw the outline of a toad. Then an almighty roar broke the silence of the night and the bridge shook as a car tore over it. It screeched to a halt at the bus stop and somebody got out and slammed the door shut behind them. 'You'd better be ready, arsehole,' said a voice I recognised. It was Dale.

I was expecting him to head straight up the hill but instead he huffed and puffed his way across the road. My heart hammered as he reached the bank of the river, just six feet away from me. I heard a zipping noise and then a splashing in the water. I was absolutely terrified. At that moment, I wished so hard that I'd never met Bea, that she hadn't got me into this and that I was anywhere but underneath a bridge, late at night, within feet of a psychopathic car dealer. Then he turned and walked back across the road but it wasn't until I heard him pushing through the bushes, on the other side, that I let myself breathe again.

140

I sat there for another ten minutes or so but I was getting more and more stiff and uncomfortable and I had no idea what was going on up on the hill. I couldn't hear anything at all so I decided to ignore Bea's instructions and I inched cautiously out from under the bridge and up the steps to the road. I stretched out my cold, cramped limbs and then crossed the road quickly and zig-zagged through the bushes to the hill. I started to walk around the bottom of it. The night was clear and fresh and, by the light of the half-moon, I saw a fox running for cover just a little way ahead of me.

Suddenly, I heard shouts. I couldn't make out the words but I knew both the voices. The shouting went on for a while and then there was a sharp ear-splitting bang and everything went quiet. I sat down, shocked. What the hell had happened? Why wasn't there any yelling or groaning or some kind of noise? The silence hung in the air for what seemed an eternity and then I heard the soft sound of someone padding gingerly down the hill.

I lay flat on my stomach and watched as a small, lean figure came into view.

'Bea,' I whispered, when she was parallel to me. 'Over here.'

She jumped. 'Shit! What are you doing here? I told you to stay under the bridge.'

'Does it matter now?' I asked.

'No,' she said, sitting down beside me. 'Nothing matters now. It's all over.'

'What happened? What was that bang?' I demanded.

'Brett shot Dale,' she said, simply.

'Shot him?' I exclaimed. 'Is he dead?'

'Yes, he's dead. I guess Brett learnt one useful thing in the army.'

'And where did he get the gun from?' I asked.

Bea didn't answer but she didn't need to. It's not like I didn't know.

We sat quietly until the cold started to bite and then we got up and started wandering along the river in the direction of town. When we got to the bridge over the deepest part of the river, we stopped and looked over. We took out our burner phones and faced the water.

'You ready?' asked Bea.

'Ready,' I said.

We hurled the phones into the water and listened as they disappeared into the depths with a satisfying plop.

'One more,' Bea said, and took another phone from her pocket.

She smashed it on the side of the railing and then dropped it into the river. 'That was Dale's,' was all she said.

It took hours to walk back and it felt like even longer. A strange, dizzying, unreal feeling came over me and my feet and legs and shoulders began to throb. When I'd imagined this walk, I'd thought that we'd have loads to talk about but we didn't. We walked in silence for most of the way. Once we reached the outskirts of the town, I checked my phone for the time. 'Five-thirty. It's still far too early for me to go home.'

'You can come with me if you want to,' said Bea.

'Where are you going?' I asked.

'Up by Ikea,' she replied.

I smiled. 'That was a good night.'

'It really was.'

'What was that song you were singing? Do you remember?' I asked.

'Of course, it's a song I've known forever.' She started to sing,

'One evening as the sun went down,
    And sleep to me was calling,
    I fell into a land that's fair and bright,
    Where no-one don't hurt you, day or night,
    Where the lemonade springs,

143

And the nightingale sings,
  In the land that's fair and bright.'

She sang all the way up the hill until we got to Ikea. We walked
round the back to the car park and Bea headed for the far wall.
I looked up at the rickety fire exit as she climbed over and then
I followed her into the cemetery.

She walked a few paces and then stopped next to a gravestone.
It was the same grave she'd stopped and leaned against when
we'd been making our great escape. I hung back as she sat down
and started to shake and to cry. 'It's over, mum,' she spluttered.
'I promised you I'd take care of it, and now I finally have.'

After a while, I sat next to her and held her tight and we cried
together. Chinks of sunlight appeared and the letters that were
carved into the gravestone became legible. There were only
two words on it – 'Sarah Tarrant.'

'What happens now?' I whispered gently, as Bea rubbed her
eyes and pulled away from me.

She grinned. 'This might sound crazy,' she said, 'but I've got
a train to catch. I'm getting the first train up to Scotland. My
aunt is expecting me.'

I stared at her. 'Wow,' I said. 'That's wonderful news and
terrible news. I'm going to miss you so much.'

'I'll miss you too,' she said. 'The last few weeks have been wild
and …'

'Terrifying?' I suggested.

'And terrifying and liberating and lots else,' Bea concluded.

'Yeah, it's been all of that,' I agreed.

We sat smiling at each other for a while and then I asked, 'How long have you got before your train goes? Do you want me to come and wave you off?'

'Not really, I kind of want to be alone now,' she said.

'I get it. I'll leave you to it.'

'Will you look out for Donna for me?' she asked, as I got up.

'Of course, I will,' I promised her. 'Goodbye, Bea.'

I rounded the church and started for home. It was eight o'clock when I finally put my key in the lock and let myself in, just about late enough for my story about staying at Andy's to stack up. Mum was just getting up. 'Everything alright with Andy?' she asked, curiously. 'You haven't fallen out, have you?'

'Andy is fine,' I smiled. 'I just missed you, that's all.' I hugged her and then we sat and ate breakfast together.

After that I went to my room and tried to message Bea on my normal phone. She'd already blocked me. That girl thought of everything.

It took a few days for all the events on the hill to become public news. Firstly, a car was reported abandoned at the bus-stop by the river, then there were reports that a distressed soldier splattered in blood had returned to the barracks late on Monday night, then a body with a gunshot wound was found at the top of the hill and, finally, the gun.

I thought mum would have a lot to say about it when she found out who the soldier was. We were sat watching the local news together when Brett's name was finally released, but she was about to go to work so we didn't have time to talk about it properly then.

The next day she was off and she asked me if I wanted to go for a walk with her. I'd arranged to meet up with Donna, though, so I couldn't. It wasn't until later that evening that we got a chance to talk about it at all.

'How was your walk?' I asked.

'It was helpful, I think. I went up to Collington Hill.'

'And what was it like up there?'

'The very top of it was fenced off and the rest of it was morbidly busy,' she said. 'It seems to have become a bit of a tourist attraction.'

'That's a bit twisted.'

She nodded and grimaced. 'How do you feel about what

happened up there?' she asked.

'Weird and glad and I don't know. It feels like it's finally over. It's not like they can let him off this one,' I said.

'That's true,' agreed mum, 'and it's good to get some kind of resolution even if it has nothing to do with us. This has been hanging over us for far too long.'

I nodded.

'They say that man he killed was quite an unsavoury character,' she continued.

'I heard that too,' I said.

THE LETTER

It was well over a year before the date of Brett's trial came round. His defence lawyer tried to get the charge changed from murder to manslaughter but the murder charge stuck. The crime looked pre-meditated. When they looked at his phone, they found he'd threatened to kill Dale, more than once. Then he'd willingly gone to meet him and taken a gun. His lawyer tried to explain that he'd found the gun at the scene but who was ever going to believe that? The prosecution had fun pointing out how far-fetched that scenario was – Brett had threatened to kill Dale, he'd gone to meet him and, as if by magic, he'd found a loaded gun at the scene – come on! It took the jury no time at all to find him guilty and the following week the judge sentenced him to twenty years.

It took me days to sort out the jumble of emotions I felt when I read all about it. The one that came out on top in the end, though, was relief. There was also jubilation and revisited anger and a little voice in my head that kept trying to tell me that I should feel guilty, but that wasn't hard to reason away. In a just world, Brett would have got a few years for what he did to me and, apart from that, he did kill Dale. No-one pulled that trigger but him.

148

The following week, I got a hand-written letter, postmarked Inverness. It was exciting to get any kind of personal letter but especially from Inverness. I tore it open and inside were four sheets of scrawly handwriting that took me a while to decipher. There was no address or date or greeting. Bea simply started off the letter stating that she'd been thinking of me since she caught the news about the sentencing, and she hoped I was okay. Then she said she probably owed me an explanation. Her writing became even wonkier at that point. This is what she said:

'Until I was five, I lived with my mum and dad. My mum was the most wonderful woman that ever lived and my dad was Dale Tarrant. My earliest memories are of him beating her and of the stories she made up whenever anyone asked her how she got her bruises. One day, my mum was downstairs and I was playing on the landing with my toys. He was lying in bed with a hangover and didn't get up until after lunch. When he did get up, he came out onto the landing, slipped on one of my toys and crashed to the ground. He was furious. He got up and started kicking me. He'd never hurt me before and I was terrified. I screamed and mum came running up the stairs. She pulled me into her arms and told him that he'd gone too far and that we were going to leave him. He grabbed her arm, shouted that that would never happen and pushed her. We went flying down the stairs together and mum's body twisted around as we dropped. She hit the ground first and I landed on top of her. He came thundering after us, paused and then leapt over us and left.

Mum was unconscious, her neck was twisted awkwardly and

blood was coming out of her head where she'd hit the wall. I got a towel from the kitchen and put it on her head to stop the blood. I kept telling her that everything was going to be okay and I sang to her like she used to do to me when I was upset. I don't know how long we stayed there like that for. He didn't come back until after it had gone dark. Then he phoned for an ambulance and said he'd just got home and found that his wife had had an accident. He wasn't sure if she was alive or not.

We followed the ambulance to the hospital. Someone must have phoned our social worker because he turned up soon afterwards. He took me into a little room and I told him what really happened. Then he took me to an emergency foster family and the next day the police came to talk to me. Over the next few weeks, I had to tell my story over and over, sometimes at the foster house and sometimes at other places. Whenever I asked, they told me my dad wasn't allowed to do that to my mum.

Then one day, the social worker and my foster mum sat me down and said that we weren't going to be seeing the police anymore and we weren't going to be going to the courthouse after all. Nobody told me why until I was thirteen. Apparently, my dad's brother had given him an alibi. He'd told the police that my dad was with him the night before my mum died, and all that day. That meant it was their word against mine and the Crown Prosecution Service decided I was too young to be taken seriously.'

After that, Bea had written, 'BURN THIS.'

Below that was a drawing of a lake surrounded by mountains. At one end of the lake was a boat with 'Monster Tours' written on the side. On the boat was a girl. She was looking at the other end of the lake where a great lizard looped out of the water. In the water were a few fishes and the words, 'My New Job.'

I read the letter through again, and then I did as she said and burned it in the sink. Next, I got my phone and looked up Monster Tours. It came up straight away and I clicked on 'Who We Are.' Half a dozen faces smiled at me and the one at the bottom was Bea. Her caption read, 'Our newest recruit has fallen in love with this beautiful area and she's a great asset to our team.'

I looked at her picture again. She looked happy.

I smiled back at her and it occurred to me that, if I knew anyone who had the patience and tenacity to find something as rare as the Loch Ness Monster, it was Bea.

About the Author

In 2020, two women found themselves in similarly traumatic circumstances. One wryly suggested to the other that they 'swap cases.' That comment was the seed for A Blighted Star. It is written under a pen name.

Printed in Great Britain
by Amazon